MARK ANCHOVY

PIZZA DETECTIVE

MARK ANCHOVY

PIZZA DETECTIVE

William Goldsmith

Piccadilly
PRESS

First published in Great Britain in 2020 by
PICCADILLY PRESS
80–81 Wimpole Street, London W1G 9RE
www.piccadillypress.co.uk

A CIP catalogue record for this book is available from the
British Library.

ISBN: 978-1-848-12861-3
Also available as an ebook and audiobook

1
Printed and bound in Great Britain by Clays Ltd, Elcograf S.p.A.

Piccadilly Press is an imprint of Bonnier Books UK
www.bonnierbooks.co.uk

To Irma and Cosmas

Exhibit A: *Girl with a Squirrel*, Leonardo da Quincy, 1513

hat I had in mind that summer was no homework and easy money. Instead, I ended up with a valuable stolen painting, various death threats and more pizza than I could handle. Perhaps I should have just done a paper round or walked someone's Labrador. But I chose to be a private detective.

It was my grandpa – G-pops – who started it. He sat there watching this grainy film starring some actor he called 'Bogey', who snooped after gangsters in a flappy cream coat.

'He's like you, kiddo,' he would rasp. 'You're

always so good at deducing things like a detective!'

By 'things', he meant deducing that the plague-puddle in his fridge was once a cucumber. Or that his glasses hadn't been kidnapped but were on his head. Or that his monthly pills had been snaffled by Dinnergloves, his dog. And that Dinnergloves needed his stomach pumped. ASAP.

'My little detective,' he would cackle, 'my little Bogey.' This might sound like a weird thing to call your grandson, but I got the reference.

For my birthday he handed me a duffed-up green-and-white paperback called *The Big Sleep* (something he was partial to). Inside the cover, alongside a library fine from 1978, he had written:

For Colin: don't ever stop being a detective.

After that, his words started pinballing around my head. I did like deducing things. Spotting things. Remembering things. The doctor once said my brain was 'like a film camera'.

What if I *was* a detective?

I mean, yes, I was a pizza delivery boy. But couldn't I be both?

A *pizza detective*?

So I got hold of a flappy cream coat. I made some laminated calling cards. I began snooping, not expecting much. After all, Rufflington-on-Sea isn't exactly a hotbed of crime. Someone might walk off with the Post Office biro. Or prank call the old phone box. Or a badger might knock over your bins.

But everything changed with one fishy password . . .

Chapter 1

t began with three suspicious pizzas. We were in Caesar Pizza, an Ancient Rome-themed pizzeria run by my parents, Cosmas and Irma Kingsley. Nice names, I know — but they went and called me Colin. Anyway, it was about eight and we were waiting for the orders to come in.

My dad was mopping up stray clouds of flour, grunting to himself. I was thinking about my school trip to Italy the next day — or trying to think, over the noise of my sister Alicia practising her double bass upstairs.

My mum babbled on the phone in her super-
polite, high-pitched voice, 'Yes, yes, Colin can
come around, yes, yes!'

She wrote down the orders and gave them to
me.

'Is that my trench coat you're wearing, darling?'
She knew it was. I just shrugged and didn't tell her
that there was no point being a detective if you
didn't have a trench coat. I read the orders:

- Major Marjorie
- Buckdean Hall, Seabury Road
- 1 x 7" Mark Anchovy Pizza, extra
anchovies

- Mr Stirling Biggs
- 40 Weeping Willow Way
- 1 x 14" Mark Anchovy Pizza,
extra anchovies

- Patrick Moore
- Hut 37, Shingle Row
- 1 x 12" Mark Anchovy Pizza, extra anchovies

For most people, this would read like a fairly harmless list of pizzas.

But if you looked closely, you would know that it was a cry for help.

'*Extra* anchovies?' said my mum, adjusting my collar as I squirmed away. 'People are funny.'

I didn't think it was funny at all. Because no one asks for extra anchovies. Unless, that is, they had seen one of these:

The cheesy, salty-fishy smell of cooked Mark Anchovy pizzas halted my train of thought.

I packed the satchel and wheeled out my bike. My dad stood in the doorway.

'Be back by nine,' he said.

'Go safely, darling,' called my mum.

'Okaaaaaaaaaaay!' I shouted, before pedalling off.

The sun was setting behind the oak trees, casting shadowy splashes on the bungalows. I picked up the pace as the tarmac blurred beneath me in a jerky flurry. I focused on my first port of call – Buckdean Hall. I'd only ever seen it from a distance, poking up from the clifftop like an elaborate tombstone. It used to be an all-girls boarding school, but we'd heard on the grapevine that someone lived there now. Who it was had been a mystery, until now. Major Marjorie . . . What kind of a name was that?

A sea mist hit my nostrils as I sped towards the

railway arches. It was cool under there, like a cave. I looked around at the traffic lights and saw a lonely kebab shop. Its neon sign, bludgeoned by a moth, spelt:

K-I-N-G---S-K-E-W-E-R

Inside was a girl with big dark eyes, rolling up wraps at lightning speed. At the till stood a bulky man wearing a paper crown. Was this the 'King'? He shouted to be heard over the din of the deep-fat fryer, 'One more lamb shawarma!'

I watched the girl as her nimble fingers flew over the pickled chillies.

A car horn honked behind me.

BEEEEEEEEEEEEEEEEEEEP!!!

Something banged against my handlebars and I capsized onto the pavement. A bus lurched past with an insulting *TOOT!* Then I saw the crime scene splattered on the kerb: my satchel had gone flying and the pizzas were everywhere. And I do mean everywhere. Quick as a flash, I peeled them off and nursed them back into their boxes.

'Holy shish, you're not actually going to serve those, are you?'

I looked up at the sneering voice. The girl had come outside, hands on hips. Her dark eyes were now especially big, glowering with disgust.

'I . . . I have to . . . I'll be late otherwise! Anyway – come on, three-second rule!'

'It's actually the no-second rule, pizza boy.'

She picked up my satchel and dusted it off with a good thwack.

The King peered out at us, adjusting his paper crown.

'Is he your dad?' I whispered.

She gave a loud, harsh cackle that got under my skin like a splinter.

'No. But you *must* call me "Princess Skewer".'

She made a throat-slitting gesture with her finger.
'Or else.'

'I'm Colin,' I mumbled as I reattached the
satchel. 'And I really need to go.'

She just shrugged. What was her problem?

I sped off, passing a procession of unnaturally
neat houses and gardens. Twilight fell and bats
squeaked overhead. Finally, I was up onto Seabury
Road, with the whole of Rufflington twinkling
below and the wind in my face. The distant waves
drummed a chaotic beat. To the left was a chalky
driveway, winding like spilt milk. I crunched up it,
and there was Buckdean Hall. Only one window
was lit, but another flashed dimly. Who'd want to
go to school here? No wonder they closed it down.

I went to grab the very-slightly-germy pizza.
But I was holding something else entirely: a King
Skewer satchel, full of kebabs!

'Pizza-heeeeeeeeeeeead!' An angry wail bounced

up the driveway. 'Princess Skewer' launched in on her bike, her ponytail swishing like a cobra. 'You took the wrong delivery, you fluff-brain!'

She whipped away the satchel and handed mine back.

'We just had to make up a whole new batch, thanks to you!'

'I'm really sorry,' I garbled. 'I don't know how –'

'What are you even *doing* in this place? No one ever comes here!'

I sighed and rattled a doorknocker shaped like an angry lion.

'Listen . . . promise to keep a secret?'

Princess raised her hand and looked solemn.

'I swear. I swear on my mum's tahini sauce.'

'I'm not really a pizza delivery boy,' I whispered, trying to inject some seriousness into my voice. 'I'm a private detective.'

Chapter 2

private detective?' yelled Princess Skewer.

'Shush!'

I was about to ask if she wanted the entire world to know when the door opened. Glaring out was a woman with sharp cheekbones and blindingly white hair.

'Mr Kingsley?' she snapped.

'Y-y-yes,' I bumbled.

'I am Major Marjorie.' She turned her head to one side. 'Are you really a private detective, young man?'

I nodded, but she didn't seem convinced.

 'And who might this young lady be?'

'Princess Skewer,' cut in Princess, offering a regal hand.

Major Marjorie took the hand as if it were a wet nappy.

'Hmph.'

'Well . . . here's your pizza,' I said, trying to break the ice. 'With extra anchovies.'

'Oh, I can't bear anchovies, Mr Kingsley, but if that's the password for your services, so be it. Come in, both of you.'

The first thing that struck me about the giant hallway was the smell. It was part lavender, part tobacco, part something else – something unpleasant.

She led us down a long wood-panelled corridor, swinging her arms like a wind-up toy soldier. Unseen clocks ticked in an agitated manner and

I counted several stuffed animals. Major Marjorie stopped and placed a trembling hand on a doorknob.

'What you are about to see, children, may shock and disturb you.'

She opened the door a fraction. 'My beloved Horace is . . . *possessed*.'

I was trying to figure out what she meant when Princess pushed me in.

Then came that smell again, but stronger – like burning plastic.

'Whoa!' cried out Princess, fanning the air.

Major Marjorie gave a long, high-pitched whimper. She was staring at a portrait above the mantelpiece. It depicted the most crazed-looking corgi dog I had ever seen. It seemed barely believable, but its eyes were actually flashing. Yes, flashing – with a mad, red glow.

'It's possessed! It's possessed, children!' Major Marjorie moancd.

'Oh, what shall I do, Mr Kingsley? Tell me!'

I tried to look at the demonic dog with the laser-beam eyes. I felt queasy, as if I might faint. Princess tugged at my sleeve.

'I think I've had enough of this, Pizza-head.'

I tried to be rational, like a proper detective. A painting couldn't be possessed, could it? Was it just a sick prank? If so, who would mess with someone who called herself 'Major'? The corgi was spooky even without the flashing eyes. Its tongue lolled out sideways and its coat was actual fur, collaged on. The eyeballs were fashioned with marbles, which had rolled in on each other to give a cross-eyed look. I took a deep breath. It was hard to think straight with this overpowering sooty smell.

'Major Marjorie, I think I've seen all I need to here.'

That sounded fairly detective-like, I thought.

'Very well, Mr Kingsley.'

I took out a pencil and scribbled some thoughts on the back of a Caesar Pizza menu.

'Oh, yes – your fee.' Major Marjorie clawed through a pile of flyers and brought out three battered pound coins.

'Is that all?' asked Princess Skewer.

'Er . . . thanks, Major Marjorie,' I cut in. 'Call Caesar Pizza tomorrow and ask for the extra anchovies again. I'll come straight away.'

'Until tomorrow then, Mr Kingsley,' said Major Marjorie, leading us out.

We were glad to be back in the fresh summer evening. Major Marjorie gave a strange mechanical wave.

'What a crank,' said Princess as we cycled away. 'Where to next?'

I didn't think it was odd that she wanted to tag along. Then again, 'thinking' wasn't my strong point that night.

The second suspicious pizza was for Mr Biggs.
You could spot his house a mile off – in fact, you
could probably spot it several miles off. You could
probably, at a stretch, even spot it from a plane.

It wasn't a distinctive building on its own. No –
what made it stand out was that every inch of it
was covered in Christmas decorations. There were
electric holly leaves, beaming snowmen and big
bright bells that rocked from side to side. There were
neon figgy puddings, flickering candy canes and
ultra-violet stockings. On the roof was the crowning
touch: a giant statue of Father Christmas with
sleigh and reindeer. This wouldn't be so unusual at
Christmas. But it was a balmy evening in June.

'Whoa,' said Princess as we approached.

'Yeah,' I said. 'They *really* like Christmas.'

We parked our bikes against a sparkling blue
igloo and rang the doorbell.

It was answered by Mrs Biggs. She wore a tracksuit and a 1980s perm.

'Did you order a Mark Anchovy pizza?' I asked.

'We did,' she whispered, looking around. 'With extra anchovies.'

'I'm Detective Colin Kingsley. This is my colleague, Princess Skewer.'

I was feeling more professional by the minute.

The hallway was cluttered up with flyers, sports jackets, studio family photos and a towering Christmas tree.

'Mr Biggs is still in bed, I'm afraid. He's recovering from the shock.' Mrs Biggs sighed. She yanked open the pizza box and wolfed down a slice. 'They chopped off his head.'

'Whose head?' cried Princess.

'It was awful,' said Mrs Biggs. 'Stirling goes up to the roof to check on Father Christmas, and some – excuse my French – snotbag, some horrible snotbag, had only gone and chopped off the reindeer's head!'

'Wowzers,' I said. 'Can we see the reindeer?'

'If it helps,' said Mrs Biggs, 'but it isn't pretty.'

She led us to the garage, where something stumpy lay covered in an old blanket. Mrs Biggs folded it back slowly.

'Oooooft.'

What we were looking at would barely qualify as a reindeer now. Robbed of its head and antlers, it was just a body made from girders, outlined in light bulbs. I fished into the trench coat and produced a pair of washing-up gloves. Yes, before you ask, they were my mum's. I touched the neck, and a fine black powder rubbed off.

'Any ideas, Pizza-head?' said Princess.

I was intrigued, but again I felt time pressing on.

'I think we'd best be going, Mrs Biggs. I shall return with more information —'

'*We'll* return with more information,' corrected Princess.

'Call Caesar Pizza tomorrow,' I continued, 'and remember to ask for extra anchovies.'

'Thanks, dearie.' She gave me a grubby fiver. 'You two best be getting home! Your parents will think you're having some kind of romance!'

'Urgh!' exclaimed Princess. 'Really, really not.'

I hoped I wasn't turning too beetroot.

'So long, Mrs Biggs.'

The third suspicious pizza was the weirdest. It was for a beach hut.

But when we reached the seafront, the hut was all boarded up with no signs of life within. I knocked and we waited, though it felt pointless.

'Obviously this is a mistake!' Princess hissed.

'Or perhaps we just missed them.' I slumped down on the doorstep.

'Great,' Princess huffed. 'Just great.'

I stared out to sea and ate a slice of the pizza, extra anchovies and all.

Somehow the water looked so much more sludge-like at night, all black and glistening. It certainly didn't invite a quick dip, not with the sound of stones being sucked up and pounded by the swell. I was halfway through my second slice when I heard a scuffling sound coming from under the pier. I stopped chewing to listen better. Princess looked at me, eyebrows raised. I ventured down and tried to be stealthy, but unfortunately Rufflington beach is a stony one. Clambering over a mound of loose pebbles gave me about as much stealth as, well, someone clambering over a mound of loose pebbles. Whatever was down there bolted for it.

I squinted and made out the outline of a small, chubby kid, pelting along the shore.

'Wait!' I yelled, and lumbered after him. 'Wait! Wait!'

The kid didn't wait. And for someone so circular he sure knew how to sprint.

'Really?' wheezed Princess, bounding along.

If he hadn't shot off like a bouncy ball, I might not have bothered. But his panic made *me* panic. Nearer the shore the stones gave way to firm sand and I was able to gain on him. But when I got close I wasn't sure about hauling him to the ground like most detectives would at this point.

'Grab his ankles!' Princess shouted.

This threat took the wind out of his sails and he cowered before us. I got the impression of an upturned nose and small, button-like eyes. I didn't recognise him from school.

'What the fluff are you doing?' moaned Princess.

'I'll handle this,' I cut in. 'Listen, mate, we were asked to deliver a pizza here and all we got was you scuttling about like a little crab.'

The boy panted and kicked a stone.

'Does your mum know you're here?'

His button eyes caught mine. 'Does yours?'

Ouch.

'Just tell me what you were up to . . . and, er, I'll give you some pizza!'

'I was just *digging* – what's your problem?'

He screwed up his face like a footballer trying to con a referee.

'Do you want that pizza, kiddo?'

'My name's Justin.' He sniffed.

'Okay, Justin – why were you digging?'

'I was sort of . . . burying something.'

'Burying what?'

He turned back towards the pier.

'You'll never know. Not now, anyway.'

An ill-fitting smile plastered itself over his chin.

The tide was coming in, and inky pools of surf

were slurping over his digging spot.

I wouldn't have bothered to find out what he had buried – it might have been a dead pet hamster or some soiled pants for all I knew. But by not telling me, he had *made* me bothered. I tore back.

'Stay here with him!'

Shining my phone, I saw a slight bump in the sand. Cold water seeped into my trainers as I squelched closer. I didn't have a spade, so I just pawed apart the sand like a mad beaver or something. A jet of foam slopped about my knees, then above my elbow. The corner of what felt like a Jiffy bag emerged from the ground. I grabbed it. Something hard and heavy was inside, but before I could think what, a bigger, nastier wave slapped me in the face. I heard the rumble of stones being sucked back and the *THOOM* of waves crashing closer. Blinking back the salt, my eyes settled on the Jiffy bag. I tugged it again.

'Pizza-head!' I heard Princess shout.

THOOM!

This time I didn't even see the wave. All I knew was that I was under one. It pinned me down, pummelling me against the stones. I tried to get up, but my legs felt like lead. The sea inhaled again, sucking me in deeper. My neck jerked violently to the side and then upward. Princess was pulling at the collar of my mum's trench coat with all her might. Our heads bobbed up and cold air buffeted into our lungs. Somehow we crawled out and slithered up the beach to safety. I looked down and realised I was still clutching the Jiffy bag.

'Thaaaaaankshh . . .' I finally gasped. 'That was a baaaad idea.'

'It was the worst idea. EVER.'

'Where's Justin?'

'Aw, shish kebab . . . he must have legged it when you went under.'

'Looks like he nabbed the pizza as well.' I groaned. '*And* the kebabs.'

I hauled myself up, then offered a hand to Princess. Her palm was calloused, but in a good way.

'Thanks, Pizza-head.'

We reached our bikes and looked back at the sea. I could have drowned out there, but now it seemed strangely quiet. Just the dim horizon and a few fairground lights still twinkling on the pier. Lights. *Wait a minute.*

'Princess – the cases – they're making sense to me now!'

'Which cases?'

'Major Marjorie and Mr Biggs, I mean. They're linked, don't you see?'

'They're both cranks, you mean?'

'No – the lights. Major Marjorie has lights randomly flashing and Mr Biggs is *missing* lights –

his electric reindeer! It must be —'

At this point Princess turned and stopped me.

'Listen, Pizza-head. Promise to keep a secret?'

'Er . . . sure,' I mumbled, taken aback.

'I'm not really a kebab vendor,' she said slowly. 'And your life is about to change forever.'

I was about to ask her what she meant, when we were caught in the headlights of a big, boxy car with a voice screaming at us from behind the wheel.

Chapter 3

'olin Kingsley! You're in big, BIG trouble!' The screaming voice was like a fire alarm that nobody knew how to turn off. How could a human being produce such a shrill, piercing sound? Yet its source was unmistakable. I felt my face burn up as the door opened and slammed and a shadowy figure bore down on us. Princess turned to me.

'Is that your mum?'

Of course it was my mum. And right now she looked like a volcano that had recently erupted and was hurling molten lava onto the villagers below.

The villagers, in this case, being me.

'What the *hell* do you think you're doing?!'
she screeched. 'You were supposed to be back at
nine! Your father and I have been worried sick!
No call, no text –' she looked at Princess '– and I
find you here, on the beach, at ten o'clock at night,
CANOODLING!'

I thought my face would melt, it was that hot.
Princess splayed her fingers in disbelief.

'Oh. My. G–'

'That's enough of that, missy! Right now, you'll
both be going home!'

'But, Mum –' I began.

'Get in the Volvo!' she screamed.

She sat Princess in the front and hauled me into
the back.

'You're soaked, Colin!'

We chugged along the deserted seafront, then over

the Eight Dials Crossroads, then past the railway arches. At King Skewer we dropped off Princess, who didn't wave goodbye. Then onto Brayne Road, the bungalows sputtering out their television-glow. I thought of all the families draining their hot chocolate before bed. I realised a) how cold I was, and b) how much I was not ready for sleep.

I looked into the wing mirror and saw my mum's face. Her anger was subsiding, and her eyes glistened with worry.

'Don't ever do that again, Colin.'

I tried to say sorry, but all that came out was a sort of hush.

We pulled up at the pizzeria and made our way up the back stairs to the flat. My dad was waiting in the hallway in his dressing gown. His skinny legs and overgrown toenails took nothing away from his deadly serious face. He gestured to the bedroom.

'Get inside,' he muttered through gritted teeth.

He perched on the edge of the bed and looked at me. My mum ripped off the wet trench coat and began buffeting me with a towel as forcefully as the waves had earlier.

'What I want to know,' my dad said slowly, 'is why Mrs Biggs phoned to ask where you were?'

I couldn't meet his intense stare, so I looked down at his toenails. Boy, they needed trimming.

'This was forty-five minutes after you set out.' He paused for effect as my mum withdrew the towel. 'Forty-five minutes,' he repeated, with gong-like clarity.

'I was . . . my bike chain came off and I was . . . delayed.'

'Again?' His gaze was burning a hole in me somewhere.

'My bike's on the blink . . .'

'Don't blame the bike, young man!' squealed my mum. 'You're lucky you even have a bike!'

'Your mum's right,' my dad added. 'The bike's not an excuse, Colin. Ten minutes to each delivery, maximum. This isn't a big town, is it?'

'Colin, listen,' said my mum, smearing on face cream. 'You need to understand. Caesar Pizza is struggling at the moment. You've seen the cracks in the walls, the leaks in the ceiling.'

The face cream looked like war paint, before she rubbed it in.

'Which means we can't afford to make customers wait three-quarters of an hour for their pizza.'

'Which means no faffing about,' said my dad.

'Cosmas –'

'What?'

'He was out . . . with a girl.'

'Urgh . . .' I groaned, and turned to leave the room.

'Get back here now,' barked my dad. 'A girl?'

'Y–yes.'

My mum was flushing slightly beneath her face cream, but my dad's stare, if I could translate it, would read: A girl? Colin? Unlikely.

'Part of me thinks we should cancel your school trip to Rome tomorrow. How would you like that?'

Actually, I wouldn't have minded that. It would just be five days of Mr Hogstein blethering on about old broken Roman stuff. My parents had somehow imagined that old broken Roman stuff would be 'good' for me.

I simply sniffed by way of an answer.

'I think it would be a real shame for you to miss that, Colin, don't you think?'

I sniffed again.

'Colin.' My mum sighed. 'It's late, and you should get to bed. But promise us you'll not let this happen again?'

'Okay.'

'Okay what?'

'Okay, I promise not to let this happen again,' I repeated like a robot.

'Don't wake up your sister.'

I left and crept into my bedroom. Alicia's snoring sounded more like a machine gun than someone who was only seven and a half years old. Right then, I wished I could be seven and a half again. I wished I hadn't signed up for possessed corgis and stolen electric reindeers and burials on beaches. And pizzas – I was sick of pizzas, too.

I slung on my pyjamas and rolled beneath the duvet, but every position I lay in felt like I was lying on a bed of nails. I remembered my dad's creased brow and my mum's worried, wet-looking eyes. Was Caesar Pizza really struggling? What would they do? I kicked off the covers, grabbed my satchel and tiptoed down to the pizzeria.

The floor gleamed with my dad's mopping.

Although he was slapdash with several things –
dressing, for instance, or buttering bread – he
always mopped floors to perfection. He'd slopped
over the browny-red tiles in slow, careful columns.
The boxes were neatly stacked, the worktops
wiped, and the tubs of toppings had been wrapped
in clingfilm and put in the big fridge.

A fan hummed peacefully. The
statue of our mascot, a toga-
wearing fish called Markus
Anchovius, watched over the
scene. Once upon a time, he
would sing a warbly tune if you
popped a coin through his mouth.
But no one did that these days.

I opened the till and shoved
in my earnings from the first day
of investigations. Eight pounds.
It wasn't much, but it was better

than nothing. Then I remembered: the Jiffy bag! It was still in my satchel, damp from its plunge.

I returned to my room, hid under the duvet and shone my phone onto the Jiffy bag.

'Coliiiiinnnnnnn,' Alicia growled.

I tore the plastic sleeve and out slid a large hardback book. It had taken a bit of a kicking from when I was underwater, but still, it looked like a fancy book. The cover was a sort of plum colour with gold lettering, which read:

The G.S.L.: A Beginner's Handbook

'Coliiiiinnnnnnn,' Alicia growled again. 'I'll tell Mum and Dad.'

'In a minute, Al.'

The pages were crinkled with damp, but I could make out diagrams and maps, and paintings of important-looking people in old-fashioned suits.

What was Justin doing
burying a book on the
beach?

'Uuurghh!' Alicia
snorted. 'I'm telling.'

'Okay, okay,' I said.

I snapped the book shut
and was just placing it on the floor when a sheet of
paper fell out. There was a weird logo in the top-
right corner, making it look quite official. This is
what it said:

*Congratulations, you've passed the first test.
Meet me in the alley.
P.S.*

P.S.: P.S. means Princess Skewer. P.S.

And this, I suppose, is where my story *really*
begins.

Chapter 4

blinked and re-read it: *Meet me in the alley.* I felt my pulse thump – did she . . . *like* me? I twitched back the curtain and peered out. At first it was hard to see Princess, but then I spotted her ponytail, curling from her head like a cartoon plume of smoke.

'Just getting a glass of water,' I whispered to Alicia. Downstairs I slung on the trench coat, gritted my teeth and prayed the back door wouldn't squeak.

'Over here, Anchovy.'

It was Princess. At that point, I didn't think to

ask why she called me 'Anchovy'.

I guess she'd been calling me 'Pizza-head' only moments earlier.

'What are you doing here? Is it because of earlier? I'm sorry if I got you into trouble, I'm really –'

'We don't have time for this, Anchovy,' she hissed. 'There's important work to be done.'

'Work? I need to sleep – I'm going on a school trip tomorrow.'

'Anchovy – this opportunity will *not* come up in your lifetime again.'

Even though I could barely see her face, I sensed she meant business. And that this was not a romantic visit. I followed her out of the alley and up Brayne Road, hurrying to keep level. Under the glare of the streetlights sat a scruffy bus. There was no bus stop, and the sign in the windscreen read NOT IN SERVICE.

'Get on,' said Princess.

'What?'

'Seriously. Get on.'

'But it says –'

'Anchovy.' Princess turned to me, and for the second time that night took my hand. 'Trust me.'

I suppose if I'd thought about it, I might have backed out. But I didn't think. I just got on, and Princess followed. I looked towards the driver, but she didn't look at me. All I saw was a head of frizzy hair and a big orange parka jacket. Pretty unofficial.

The bus juddered into gear and wove its way through Rufflington.

'Save your questions for later,' said Princess. 'It will save everyone a lot of time.'

Everyone?

We were soon on the outskirts of town, a sorry stretch of tarmac covered in empty bulldozers. I could see the old bowling alley, Lightning

Strikes. I think my mum and dad had their first date there back in the day – but it's abandoned now. The frizzy-haired driver slowed to a halt. Princess motioned for me to get off and I looked around. There were barricades everywhere and construction signs saying KEEP OUT and DANGER. Again, there was no bus stop. Just a pile of rubble and a fluorescent yellow sign that read:

KNOTTING SURFACE

'Knotting surface?' I said out loud. I looked back at the bus. Oh. *Not in service.* 'I get it. Very good.'

'Over here, Anchovy.'

Princess crawled through a perfect square hole, like a rabbit hutch, in the wire-mesh fence. I followed and we walked towards the bowling alley. It's an odd, blocky building with wonky lettering. I'm sure when it was built it looked 'modern'. Now it just looks a mess. Princess pushed open some double doors with circular windows and we entered a hallway tiled like a chessboard. On my right hung photos of people in triangular glasses and trousers up to their armpits. One caption read: *Rufflington Ten Pin Bowls Team 1957.* On my left was a dusty rack with black-and-red trainers. Princess put some on.

'Get a pair,' she whispered.

'Are we actually going bowling?'

She tugged her laces and glared at me. 'What do you think this is, Anchovy? A *date?*'

I reached for a pair of sevens and squinted up ahead. At the end of the dim hallway stood a robed figure with his back to us. His slicked-down hair shone in the light of a vending machine. From somewhere, the murmur of a crowd began to grow in volume.

'Anchovy,' Princess said, raising her voice, 'I'd like you to meet someone very important. His name is Master Key.'

Now we were closer, I could see that his robe was in fact a silk dressing gown. His feet were clad in sequined slippers. He turned around.

'Mr Anchovy.'

I had been expecting a creepy older man – but he was only a few years older than me. He had an almond-shaped face with multicoloured eyes; one was brown, the other blue.

'I am Master Key. Branch President of the G.S.L.' His voice was somehow soothing.

'The G.S.L.?' I asked.

'The Golden Spatula League.'

I noticed the pattern on his dressing gown – repeated yellow cooking spatulas on a crimson background. 'You won't have heard of us. We are the greatest organisation of catering detectives in existence. Welcome.'

He waved a jewel-studded hand towards the

bowling alleys. I was expecting a big dusty space with crooked floorboards and broken glass. Instead, I found myself staring with my mouth wide open. Before me lay about a dozen bowling lanes, each with a long narrow table stretching to the skittle pits. Seated at these were hundreds of kids, chattering away. They were wearing uniforms of some sort – though not matching uniforms. They looked roughly my age. It was like a school canteen but without a single adult in sight. Plus, it was a bit more up-market than our school canteen. The tables were laid out for the biggest fancy dinner party I had ever seen. There were purple tablecloths, crimson-edged white napkins and gold-coloured spatulas arranged in diamond shapes. What was up with all the spatulas?

Master Key floated to the head of a table. Princess sat on his left and nudged me to sit opposite.

'Please forgive my rudeness, Anchovy,'
said Master Key. 'Our conference feast is at
Rufflington-on-Sea this season, and we thought it
was the perfect opportunity to welcome you. We
have been monitoring you for some time.'

'Me?'

'Yes, Anchovy. You. We have followed your
every movement.'

'Every movement?'

I was hoping this didn't mean when I beat-box
while brushing my teeth.

'We know a lot about you, Anchovy.'

'Don't look scared!' sneered a voice across from
me.

I looked up and nearly fell off my chair. It was
Justin, that pesky kid from the beach. His doughy
head was barely above the table.

'What are *you* doing here?'

'I'm a detective for the G.S.L., like,' said Justin.

He winked and made a mock gun out of his finger and thumb. 'So back off, fish-breath.'

'Juice Box, or Justin, as you might know him,' said Master Key, 'is apprenticing for the G.S.L.' He looked at Justin. 'An apprentice, not a detective, Juice Box. You can also be an apprentice, Anchovy. Very possibly a detective one day, too.'

'So can I!' shouted Justin, but he was ignored. Princess piped in.

'The thing is, Anchovy, those three cases were all, well, fake. Sorry.'

'Fake?' I bawled. 'No, they weren't!'

'I like your fighting spirit, Anchovy,' said Master Key. 'But Princess is right. Nudging you off your bike, swapping the satchels – all routine manoeuvres that we can of course train you in. The three cases were, shall we say, "tests". Rigging the corgi, stealing the reindeer and, finally, burying the handbook on the beach. We needed to test both your wits and your physical endurance.'

I slumped back in my seat.

'But you passed these tests with flying colours.'

'With a little help from me, Master Key . . .' chipped in Princess.

'Yes, well, that's to be expected for a novice,' said Master Key. 'Anchovy – tell us: what did you make of those cases?'

I sat up and concentrated. I closed my eyes and thought of the pictures that were in my head. I separated them and studied them like film stills. *Colin's brain is a bit like a film camera*, the doctor had once said to my parents.

'Well – there was something strange about the smell in Major Marjorie's house,' I began. 'Like the smell of a bonfire, kind of sooty – and a bit plasticky. I thought perhaps it was something to do with the fire – or the chimney. Perhaps it wasn't the picture that was flashing red, but something inside the chimney, *behind* the corgi? And that something was the head of the reindeer that was missing from the Biggs' rooftop. Am I right?'

Master Key was smiling kindly.

'And wait –' I said, another film still appearing in my brain. 'Both the Biggs and Major Marjorie had flyers in their hallway, advertising a chimney sweep – a chimney sweep! That's how you got it in there!'

'I was right, Princess – this kid's good,' said Master Key. 'What you've demonstrated, Anchovy, is that you qualify *perfectly* for the Golden Spatula League. Everyone here has two things in common. First: they all work in a part-time catering job. Second: they all have a freakish skill.' He waved towards the other tables. 'Mine is infiltration. I can smuggle you into anywhere. And I mean anywhere.

Whatever the security, whatever the situation. I work as a private sushi chef, hired by exclusive clients.'

'I can run fast!' shouted Justin. 'And I can –'

'Yes, Juice Box. We know all that.'

Master Key nodded at two girls with pink-and-blue dyed hair.

'See those identical twins? Yaconda and Yelena.'

I wasn't sure about 'identical'. Anyone could see that Yelena's dimple was a good seven millimetres longer than Yaconda's.

'They're exposed to customers purely through their voices: they're world-class impressionists. Any voice – male or female, tenor or falsetto, husky or reedy – they can do it.'

The twins looked at me and smiled.

'Pleased to meet you, Mr Anchovy!'

I froze. They were speaking in my voice – perfectly. Master Key chuckled.

'They're also fluent in several languages. Any time we need to make a fake phone call, the twins are on it.'

He then pointed to a boy with a cloud-shaped puff of hair. He seemed to be excavating the contents of his nostrils.

'That's Camillo. Italian supernerd.'

I watched him study the snot on his fingernail, then wipe it on the tablecloth.

'He'll hack us into any closed network and pick up all online correspondence,' said Master Key. 'Frankly, I don't know why anyone would spend that kind of time staring at a computer screen. He also builds robots.'

'My skill,' said Princess, 'is forgery. Started in school when I did people's sick notes. Any fake documentation needed for the G.S.L., I provide.'

I remembered her fast, nimble fingers speeding over the shawarma wrap.

'And yours, Anchovy,' said Master Key, 'is your memory. You have an extraordinary gift.'

'You mean my brain like a film camera?'

'Yes – it could help us gather vast amounts of information. Plus, as a pizza-delivery-boy-private-detective – or 'pizza detective,' shall we say? – you fit perfectly.'

'What's with all the catering stuff? Why can't you just be detectives?'

Master Key sighed and looked at Princess.

'Think about it, Anchovy,' said Princess. 'We're invisible.'

'No one ever notices a waiter, a steward or a chef,' continued Master Key. 'People see a faceless pair of hands, serving them food.'

'Let's say there's a super-swanky hotel,' said Princess. 'There's a diamond smuggler staying there. Or a corrupt football official. Or a wannabe president assassin.'

'That's a dangerous hotel.'

'Shut up and listen. Who's going to have access to all those people? Not the police. Not a spy pretending to be a hotel guest. No. But the catering staff will. They're the people who deliver room service at three in the morning. The people at that diamond smuggler's shoulder, piling on the croissants while he makes notes on his napkin. The invisible people.'

'And everyone always trusts children,' said Master Key. 'Which is, of course, a mistake.'

'You got the *G.S.L. Beginner's Handbook*,' said Princess. 'Everything is in there.'

'When are we eating?' hollered Justin.

Master Key rolled his eyes, rose from his seat and clapped his hands. The entire bowling alley fell silent.

'Friends. You have travelled far and wide to this sleepy little town. Welcome.'

Yelena and Yaconda stood up and repeated this line in French, Italian, Spanish, Russian, Japanese, Greek and several other languages. It took a while. Master Key then continued in English.

'Today we welcome a new apprentice – Mark Anchovy!'

A hundred pair of eyes stared at me and I felt my face turn beetroot. It was way worse than the time I farted in assembly.

'My name's Colin,' I whispered to Master Key.

He ignored me.

'It is late, friends, and I will cut the waffle. All I will say is welcome to our new apprentice, and remember, *aureum in spatha est, vivat spatha!*'

My school didn't do Latin – or whatever this was – but it made all the kids whoop and raise their drinks. These were cans of fizz, which they started shaking and spraying like Formula One drivers. Then I heard a solid clunk at my side. It was a bowling ball, which had rolled back up the conveyor belt and into the little machine at the top.

'Grab one,' said Princess.

I put my middle finger and thumb into the holes and lugged up a bubblegum-pink ball. Princess grabbed a red one with white swirls.

'Open it.'

I looked closely – there was a slit along the side of the ball. I put my hand on the top half and twisted. It came off, revealing a neatly divided set of compartments. In each of these were different food items: little slices of pizza, some party-style sausage rolls, a mini fruit salad and a lower tier of jelly sweets.

'It's a bit like a bento box,' said Master Key. 'Please eat.'

What with all the excitement, I had grown pretty hungry. Everyone tucked in to their bowling-ball bento boxes. Some people – like

Justin – grabbed a second or even a third bowling ball.

I felt relieved that we were all just gobbling down the food – some kids were catching up and had taken their eyes off me at last. I overheard little snippets:

'Been out in Budapest for the ambassador. Serving goulash to some gangsters.'

Or,

'New York, yep. Trust me, don't ever eat those street pretzels. I was undercover and saw one vendor pee in the oil. Doc swap at the Knicks stadium.'

Or,

'It was tough. Assassination attempt at the Sydney Opera House. Had to intercept some poisonous canapés.'

These 'caterer detectives' seemed to travel around, I thought.

Eventually the empty balls were rolled back into the skittle pit — I guess there was a team of people underneath the lanes. Soon everyone was tilting back in their plush chairs and burping happily. Master Key dabbed his mouth with a napkin and turned to me.

'May we have a word with you in private, Anchovy?'

Chapter 5

aster Key and Princess led me to a little kiosk at the back. I guessed that this was the cash office in the glory days of the bowling alley. Inside were three chairs and a small writing desk. On this lay a fountain pen, a pot of purple ink and a bowling ball. Master Key sank into a battered swivel chair and invited me and Princess to sit. On the wall behind him were gold spatulas, arranged in a diamond shape.

'How are you, Anchovy? A lot to take in, isn't it?'

'Yeah, my head is sort of hurting a little.'

'I'll keep it brief.'

He opened up the bowling ball and pulled out a small gold teapot.

'Tea?'

'Erm . . . okay.'

He placed a steaming cup before me. It smelt more like perfume than tea. He then brought out a folder of papers.

'We would like to formally invite you to join the Golden Spatula League. You would begin as an apprentice caterer detective, with Princess Skewer as your supervisor. I'd be your mentor and manager.'

I nodded, dazed.

'This is a dangerous existence, Anchovy. We will respect your decision if you choose to decline.'

'The money's good, though,' said Princess.

'Your salary is highly desirable,' agreed Master Key. 'G.S.L. members normally retire at sixteen, and generally don't need to work again.'

'We're talking big bucks,' said Princess. 'Plus, you get to travel all over the world.'

'But we expect a lot of you, Anchovy,' said Master Key firmly. 'Let me stress – this is a privately funded organisation which cooperates with the most powerful people in the world.'

I laughed, but for the first time that evening, Master Key frowned. He held up a ringed finger.

'Anchovy – do not take this lightly. The first rule of the G.S.L. is to take nothing at face value. Laugh if you like. But soon you'll realise that having your life at stake is no laughing matter.'

'I'm sorry.'

'Do you accept this offer, Anchovy? Will you choose the way of the G.S.L.? Will you become a caterer detective and live a life of both luxury and immense danger?'

I stared at the wall behind him, at the mounted spatulas. I thought of the life I had known, only twenty-four hours earlier. Ancient-history homework. Packing for the school trip. Delivering fishy pizzas. I thought of my parents, how worried they were when I stayed out late. But what would happen if I said no? If I never saw the G.S.L. again? I might end up delivering pizzas all my life. And my detective work in Rufflington wasn't really going places. The Biggs and Marjorie cases weren't even real.

I looked at Princess Skewer. She widened her big dark eyes at me.

'Well?'

I gulped.

'I'll accept.'

Princess smiled and looked at Master Key.

'We are delighted,' he said, and sipped his fragrant tea. 'Please sign here.'

He slid across the papers and fountain pen.

'What's this?'

'Your contract and first assignment. Starting immediately.'

'Okay . . .' I said.

'We want you to go to Italy.'

'I'm going to Italy anyway.'

'And when you get there, we want you to deliver pizzas.'

'So, basically what I'm doing now, only in Italy?'

'No, Anchovy. This will be very different.'

'Okay, but my name's Colin.'

'No, your name will be Mark Anchovy. Within this organisation. You must forget your old name.'

I looked down at the contract. It seemed too late to turn back now. I uncapped the pen and signed, in purple ink:

Mark Anchovy

I never liked the name Colin anyway.

'Excellent,' said Master Key, 'but there is just

one more thing.' He brought out a thin sheet of paper, perforated into tiny sections. 'Take off your left shoe, please.'

'What? Why?'

'We are giving you a tattoo.'

'I – I – was that in the contract?'

'Somewhere in the small print, yes. Don't worry. We only use temporary tattoos for apprentices.'

I heaved a sigh of relief, removed my shoe and peeled off my sock. I saw Princess suppress a laugh when I brushed out some bits of fluff.

'Nice toe-jam.'

Master Key tore off a section of paper and pressed it against the inside of my second toe.

'This is your special mark – you could call it *the* Mark Anchovy. Show this in times of crisis and a G.S.L. member will come to your aid.' He rubbed the transfer on, his multicoloured eyes locked in concentration.

'There.'

It was a small but recognisable image of Markus Anchovius, the mascot at Caesar Pizza. A happy-looking fish in a toga.

'*The* Mark Anchovy,' I whispered. I'd never had a tattoo before.

Master Key shook my hand, then leaned back and crossed his slippered feet on the desk.

'Congratulations, Anchovy. It has been a real pleasure to meet you. Princess will escort you home now. She will give you more information on your assignment.'

The three of us wandered back past the lanes and along the chequered-tiled corridor. I changed out of my bowling shoes.

'I will say goodbye here, Anchovy,' said Master Key. 'I must stress again – forget your old name. It would be incredibly dangerous to call you by it. Dangerous for everyone.'

Princess and I headed to the bus. The same driver was at the wheel. Once again, she didn't say a word to us. I chewed over Master Key's last comment: *Forget your old name . . . it would be dangerous for everyone.* It was only until much, much later that I would know what he meant.

The bus rumbled into gear and I watched the bowling alley fade from view. Rufflington at two in the morning seemed dead to the world. Princess, however, was still bouncing off the walls.

'Here's the deal, Anchovy. We're combining your school trip to Italy *with* this mission. Okay?'

'Er . . .'

'You do your school trip in the daytime, got it? Do your museums and ruins and stupid little worksheets. When everyone's gone to bed you come to us.'

I sensed that working for the G.S.L. meant sleep went out of the window.

'We need you in Rome to deliver pizzas to a mastermind criminal we've been monitoring. Big Alan Fresco. He's under house arrest for the suspected robbery of a famous painting. And he's got an addiction to pizzas.'

The bus lumbered onto Brayne Road.

'Just deliver his pizzas and observe him,' said Princess. 'Note down anything strange. Think you can handle that? The Italian government has called us in on this, so no pressure.'

I nodded, too stunned to comment. The bus stopped and the doors hissed open.

'We'll pick you up at your hotel. We have all the details.'

I made some kind of agreeing sound and waved her goodbye.

See you in Rome! she mouthed, before the bus drove off.

I crept through the side door of Caesar Pizza

and up to my room. I slept terribly.

I dreamt of crashing waves and bowling alleys and stolen paintings. What had just happened to me? And who in the world was Big Alan Fresco?

Chapter 6

woke up spluttering and shaking. Then I realised – it was the *bed* that was shaking.

In my daze I sensed a tall, broad figure looming above me. I shrank back into the duvet and groaned.

'Eeeeeeeeeeeeeeeeeeeurgh!'

The bed continued to shake.

'Go away . . .' I croaked. 'Go away. Please.'

'Coliiiiiiiiiiinnn . . .'

I froze. Slowly, I made a tiny opening in the duvet like a porthole, which allowed one eyeball to peer out.

'Get up get up get up get up!'

I saw my sister's cheeky
face, her darting eyes framed
by the wonky fringe she'd
cut herself. I stuck the rest
of my head out and rubbed
my eyes. It was still the same old room.
Our posters and beanbags and socks strewn about,
with comics lying open like half-eaten sandwiches.
Maybe there was a half-eaten sandwich in here
somewhere, too. The figure looming above me was
just Alicia's double-bass case. The shaking was just
her fists, pounding at my bedhead.

'Get up get up get up get up!' she snapped.

I couldn't get up, but I could at least sit up.

'Mum says eat this.'

She wafted a plate of hot buttered crumpets
under my nose and handed me tea in my Tintin
mug.

'Then get downstairs. Like, now. Actually, like, ten minutes ago.'

'Mfff?' I said, not bothering to wipe the waterfall of melted butter from my chin.

'Seriously,' said Alicia.

In the kitchen, dressed, refreshed and crumpetted, I was given a sharp nudge in the ribs.

'Soooo . . .' purred my mum. 'Do you want to tell me about this girlfriend of yours?'

'She's not my girlfriend.'

I faffed with the trench coat.

'Sorry, darling. This girl-who-is-a-friend of yours. What's her name?'

'Er . . . Princess Skewer.'

'Princess? Oh, I'm not sure about that. You can't go around calling yourself "Princess".'

'No . . . it's a sort of . . . nickname.'

'How sweet. You mean like a pet name? Like "honeybun" or "shnookums" or "babykins" or something?'

'Well, no, not really, Mum. I –'

'Irma! We need to get going!' called my dad.

'Well, don't just stand there then, put his suitcase in the car, Cosmas!'

The next six hours were so boring that my night of being a superstar detective seemed like it never happened. My parents dropped me off in the playground and I joined up with the other kids. None of them seemed nearly as cool as the G.S.L.

Our suitcases were piled into the coach and we trawled up to the airport.

Mr Hogstein and Miss Odedra gave us their usual lecture. About health and safety, about sticking together, about not talking to any strangers. Which seemed ironic, given that I was about to get cosy with a world-renowned criminal.

Yawning uncontrollably, I soon drifted off.

I must have trudged through the airport like a zombie. I remember stirring to life on the plane. My classmate Robin was on my right, drooling in his sleep. On my left, clouds spilled below me like fluff from a ripped-up soft toy. I could see the big bald dome of Mr Hogstein a few seats in front. How I'd love to have chucked something at it. Just then I heard the squeak of trolley wheels and began fumbling for some euros.

'Please take a menu, sir.'

I looked up at the voice. Staring back at me, in a black-and-orange uniform, necktie and badge, with her hair in a bun, was Princess Skewer.

'How did you —?'

'Any drinks, refreshments or snacks, sir?'

Play it cool.

'Erm . . .'

The menu seemed to weigh a ton. I opened it up and a thick, pale-blue envelope fell out. The

G.S.L. logo was stamped in gold on the front.

'I'll have an orange juice, please!' I said, but Princess Skewer – or Tracy, as her badge said – was wheeling the trolley away.

'Get it yourself,' she called back. Some of the other kids heard this and laughed.

Master Key was right. He could get anyone into anywhere – G.S.L. detectives working as air stewards! I tore open the envelope. I recognised the purple ink of Master Key's fountain pen. The letter inside read:

Apprentice Caterer Detective Mark Anchovy
Seat 33C, Flight EZY8251
Somewhere over the Alps

The Golden Spatula
League
Undisclosed Location

Dear Mr Anchovy,

Please read this letter carefully before immediately destroying it. The following methods of destroying said letter are recommended, in order of reliability:

Either,

a) Tear the letter into tiny pieces, conceal in tissue, then flush down the on-board toilet.

b) Tear the letter into tiny pieces and conceal in the mashed potato of the lunch of the boy next to you. He has been given a mild sedative and will be out for several hours.

c) Tear the letter into tiny pieces and conceal in your underpants, before removing to burn the pieces at a later date.

(The choice is yours.)

The purpose of this letter is to brief you about your assignment, codenamed **Operation Stuffed Crust**.

You are required to track the movements, behavioural patterns and any correspondence of Mr 'Big Alan' Fresco. Here are some important **facts about Mr Fresco:**

- He is a known art thief/forger who has served time in prison.
- He now resides in Villa Campino, Rome.
- His real name is Alan Fraser and he is originally from Milton Keynes.
- He is under house arrest, and never leaves his private steam room.
- He is suspected of stealing the painting 'Girl with a Squirrel" by the fifteenth-century artist Leonardo da Quincy.
- This painting is worth something in the region of 20 million US dollars.
- Mr Fresco is an extremely well-nourished gentleman and orders a pizza every evening.

- He HATES anchovies.

Hates anchovies? Already I didn't like him. I read on:

Your assignment:

As a pizza detective, you will work undercover at Mr Fresco's favourite pizzeria, La Casa Bianca. Each evening in Rome, you will deliver a pizza to Mr Fresco.

Converse with him while he eats. Learn what you can about him. Befriend him, if need be. Note down any reference to paintings he has come into contact with. Be especially vigilant over any communication he tries to make with the outside world.

It is likely that this will contain information on the whereabouts of *Girl with a Squirrel*.

Your point of communication:

Princess Skewer, Lead Caterer Detective

Gelateria Il Delfino

Salita XX Settembre

Rome

ITALY

Your deadline:

This approaching Saturday, 15 June.

Good luck with your assignment.

Please destroy this letter.

Yours Sincerely,

M.K.

I looked up, hoping for a glimpse of Princess. She had vanished behind the curtain at the back of the plane. I re-read the letter, then took a mental photograph of its contents. I tore it up into tiny pieces. I didn't have the heart to hide them in Robin's mashed potato, so I got out to flush them down the toilet. I returned to my seat, climbed over the sleeping Robin and dug out my G.S.L. handbook.

I'd just begun reading about the Golden Spatula League and its founding in 1867 when I was interrupted by Hogstein.

'Boys and girls, ahem! Ahem! We are now approaching Rome!'

He was doing his usual snorefest at the front of the plane.

'Does anyone know how the city of Rome was founded?'

No hands went up.

'It was founded by twin boys, abandoned at birth. They were called Romulus and Remus. How did they survive, children?'

Still no hands went up.

'They were raised by a she-wolf! In this statue you will see the twins,' he pointed to a print-out, 'suckling on the wolf's teats – stop giggling, Dexter!'

'What did you say, sir?'

Thankfully he was interrupted by the captain's voice, announcing that we were about to land. I closed the handbook and tried to think about my assignment. Befriend a notorious criminal?

Hogstein herded us through the airport and made us all wear these stupid matching fluorescent caps so they wouldn't lose us. Then he wasted another chunk of time by calling the register over and over again. Then he rolled out what he thought was some pretty slick Italian to the bus driver. It wasn't. It was just Hogstein shouting in English with a bad Italian accent, waving his hands around. Eventually we were off, a busload of twenty-nine hyperactive school kids and one very tired pizza detective. We wound up in a hotel that leant dangerously to one side on a winding, hilly street. It looked how I felt: knackered. The view was a big patchwork stretch of orangey-red rooftops, with TV aerials cluttering the sky like lots of little insect legs. We could see someone's washing, hear the clang of a bell, the yapping of dogs. It all seemed to wobble in the heat. I was sharing a stuffy room with six other boys. They had their football stickers out and had shoved their stinky feet into oversized flip-flops. Hogstein knocked on the door to announce that dinner would be in one hour.

Enough time, I thought, to have a nap. I unzipped my suitcase for a change of T-shirt. But where I expected to find my neatly packed clothes was something else: a small human body.

Chapter 7

screamed and it wriggled to life, turning its head towards me.

'SURPRISE!!'

'Justin!! What the *heck*?'

'How's it going, Anch, all right?' He unbent his stocky limbs out of my suitcase.

'What are you doing here? How did you get in my suitcase? Where are my pants?'

'Whoa, whoa. One question at a time, Anchovy. You didn't think you could fit me *and* your pants in there, did you?'

'I didn't ask for you to come along. I bet nobody

asked you to come along!'

'Easy, tiger. That's
harsh, that is. I
come along to help
you on this mission,
volunteering, like, and
you blow a gasket?'

'Shut up, Justin! Do you realise . . . ?'

The boys in the room had put down their
football stickers and were staring at us.

'Dude,' said Robin. 'Was that kid in your *suitcase*?'

'I – I . . .'

The other boys starting whispering and shooting
each other worried looks. I'm pretty sure I heard
someone say, 'I'm telling Hogstein.' Justin twiddled
his thumbs. He didn't seem to mind that he'd
landed me with the mother of all headaches.

'It's fine, guys, he's . . . I don't know this kid . . .'

'Mr Hogsteeeeeeein!!' Dexter squealed. 'Help!

Help!'

In a flash, they had all piled on Justin, pinning him down.

'Get off him!' I shouted.

There was a knock at the door.

I stood rooted to the spot. Dexter answered, but it wasn't Mr Hogstein. It was only a chambermaid, carrying a tray piled so high with plates, jugs and other bits that we couldn't even see her head.

'I'll run and get Hogstein,' said Dexter. But before he could, the chambermaid swung her heel at the door, slamming it shut. She put the tray down, and we saw her face. Princess. Again.

'*Servizio in camera?*' she called out. Then, in a convincing Italian accent, 'Room service?'

The boys were stunned. So much so that they released Justin, who slithered towards her on his belly. Princess then took out a can of Febreze and sprayed the air liberally.

I guess with eight boys in there, it must have stunk.

'You two –' she beckoned to me and Justin '– this way, please.'

She led us outside, slammed the door behind her and opened a laundry cupboard. She pushed me in, and practically booted Justin in after me.

'WHAT THE FLUFF ARE YOU PLAYING AT?!!!' she hissed.

Like most laundry cupboards, it wasn't the largest space, and I could feel her breath hot on my face. I wished she liked me.

'I can't believe this. Juice Box! No one told you could come, you hear? No one!'

'I – I was only trying to help, Princess.'

'Not good enough! Do you know how expensive it is to monitor *one* apprentice in a case like this, let alone two?'

'He meant well, Princess.'

'Shut up, Anchovy! This is just as much your fault! How could you not realise there was an actual person in your suitcase?'

'Okay, I'm sorry. But I think we should stop those boys before they tell Hogstein.'

'I drugged them, it's okay.'

'Drugged them?'

'That wasn't Febreze. It's fine – they'll pass out, forget everything, then wake up in time for tea.'

'Nice work, Princess!' snivelled Justin. His attempted high-five was met with thin air.

'Listen, Juice Box. We're sending you home. We can't have two apprentices working on this case . . . Master Key is going to be so fluffing annoyed with you.'

Justin hung his head.

'Both of you!' she added, looking at me.

We crept back into the hall.

'I'll take care of him,' Princess said. 'Go back to

your room, open the windows and eat your spag bol with everyone else later. Someone will collect you after lights out.'

'Thanks, Princess. I'm sorry, again.'

'We can't have any more fluff-ups, Anchovy.'

She grabbed Justin by the scruff of his neck and marched him out of a side door.

I felt miserable at the meal later, and it wasn't just because of the fly exploring my bolognese sauce. I had got off to a terrible start. I was sure that the G.S.L. would fire me. How could I let Justin smuggle himself into my suitcase? How did he even manage it? To give him credit, that was skilful. But he'd nearly blown my cover. If it hadn't been for Princess . . .

After the meal the teachers explained our schedule for the trip.

'Tomorrow, boys and girls,' waffled Hogstein,

'we will be going to a place called the Colosseum. Can anyone here tell me what that is?'

Silence.

'Anyone?'

More silence. Some giggling at the back.

'You all know about gladiators, don't you?'

A few boys looked up from their spaghetti and nodded.

'Well, the Colosseum was where gladiators fought each other with swords and spears and chains, in front of the Roman emperor!'

Hogstein scraped back his chair and began to swing his arms around. I suppose he was trying to mime being a gladiator.

'These men were wild, wild! They would stab and scratch and gouge each other's eyes out . . .'

'Cool!' called Dexter.

'Imagine the scene, children – blood and guts everywhere.'

I looked down at my bolognese and felt sick.

'Imagine if that was *your* job, children. Think yourselves lucky that you don't have to maim and shred each other to pieces!'

'Please, Arnold,' I heard Miss Odedra whisper to Hogstein. He carried on.

'Who was the winner of these fights, children? The last man standing, that's who. These men fought to the death! The death!'

'Woooooooooo!' Dexter and his gang were whooping and clapping. Idiots.

I looked over at Robin. He was still semi-drugged, I think.

Miss Odedra took over.

'Thank you, Mr Hogstein, for that, erm, *spirited* re-enactment. I hope you will enjoy tomorrow's history lesson, children. The Colosseum is a dazzling feat of architecture. Thankfully there will be no blood and guts to see on *our* visit!'

We trudged up to the dorm and I flopped onto my bed. When my head hit the pillow, it didn't make the soft plop I was expecting. It made a sort of crinkling sound. I sat up and saw a folded sheet of paper. Another note? It wasn't the most cleverly hidden. I picked it up and looked over at the other boys. They were laughing and farting and doing impressions of different cartoon characters. I unfolded the note and read:

NeXt TIMe Youll Be SleepIng With The AnChoVies.

The expression is normally 'sleeping with the fish' but I'd seen enough gangster films to know what 'sleeping with the anchovies' meant. It meant being chucked into the sea and being forced to stay there. In short, this was a death threat.

The letters were all cut out and glued on. An old-fashioned and impractical approach to death threats – even I could see that. But who could have done this? Not the boys in the dorm. We'd all been downstairs a few minutes ago, slurping spaghetti. And it couldn't be someone in the G.S.L. While I knew I would get a warning for Justin smuggling himself into my suitcase, the punishment wouldn't be death. Plus, letters from the G.S.L. had always been more formal – the blue paper, the gold seal, the purple ink flourishes of Master Key. Who had taken the time to write this? How did they know where I was?

I was distracted by Dexter flipping the light switch up and down.

'Strobe! Strobe!' he gibbered. 'Unce-unce-unce.'

'GET THAT LIGHT OFF, YOUNG MAN!' screamed Hogstein from the corridor. The room was plunged into darkness. All was quiet except for the odd fart and hiss of deodorant.

As you'd expect for a twelve-year-old who had

just received their first threatening note, I didn't sleep particularly well. I dreamt I was locked in a suitcase, banging my fists to get out. I felt something nudge me and opened my eyes. It was Princess, standing over me in a long blue jacket, a finger to her lips.

'Get dressed.' She handed me a bundle. It was a wetsuit.

'What is this?'

'Just put it on.'

I slipped it on under the sheets, flapping like a total moron.

Out in the corridor, Odedra and Hogstein were pacing around like dopey hens. We waited for them to reach the far end. Princess had brought up a cleaner's trolley, which she spun around to form a sort of screen. We then crawled towards the chambermaid's door at the other end of the corridor. We descended a spiral staircase and I showed Princess the note.

'Did you guys write this?'

She frowned but looked nonplussed.

'It's a death threat. You'd better get used to these. After a while some of them are quite funny.'

'But – who was it? Why?'

'I don't know, Anchovy! I'm not a machine! It's bad news, though.'

'Thanks for pointing that out.'

'Listen – remember who's the supervisor here. Less of that lip.'

I sighed, remembering the fake cases in Rufflington. *I'd* been the detective then and she was just tagging along. Now it was the other way around.

We wandered out of a back door and crossed a small car park.

'Do you think it's Big Alan Fresco?'

'No, Anchovy. There's no way he'd know about

you. Have you even left the hotel yet?'

I shook my head.

'We'll analyse the note and get to the bottom of this.' She looked at me and widened her eyes. 'Don't worry. The G.S.L. always gives full protection to its members. Especially apprentices.'

That was all well and good, I thought. I still didn't feel great receiving a death threat, then wandering around a foreign city at night. In a wetsuit.

'Where are we going?'

'You'll see. Not far.'

I'd expected secret lanes and alleyways, but we were walking through a busy main street, with taxis tooting angrily. The street sloped upwards, and we broke away from the traffic. We came to a square dominated by an impressive fountain, which felt familiar. It was practically deserted except for a smooching couple.

'Recognise this? Trevi Fountain. It's pretty famous. It's always best seeing it at four in the morning, when no one's around. Well –' she looked at the smoochers '– *nearly* no one's around.'

She coughed loudly. The couple parted in a web of saliva and frowned at us. Princess frowned back. Feeling the full force of the Skewer-stare, the couple linked arms and stumbled away. I looked at the fountain – I could see why it was famous. It was backed by a vast wall of pillars and archways. The fountain was on several tiers and covered with statues – mostly horses with wings and big bearded men blowing through shells. As you do.

We approached the water, which sparkled with the silver and copper of coins chucked in. Princess took off her jacket to reveal a wetsuit like mine.

'Wait a minute . . . we're not . . .'

'I hope you're good at holding your breath.'

'No, Princess, I'm not –'

'Get in, Anchovy, you big wimp.'

'No!'

'Fine. Just stay here then.'

And before I knew what was happening, she'd plunged in and soaked me.

'Princess!'

She glided to the floor where all the coins were. In the wobble of the water I could see her finger press one of the coins. When she did this the floor of the fountain began to judder and shake. Like a great yawning whale's mouth, a section opened into a large circle and Princess swam through. I blinked and looked again. I'd seen some pretty weird things this week. This was topping it. Just then I heard voices nearby. Maybe it was the smooching couple again. Maybe it was the police. I didn't want to find out, so I had no other option. I dived in.

Chapter 8

he water was as cold and gross as it looked. I opened my eyes and saw the sparkling coins and the opening that Princess had swum through. Her head appeared and she beckoned frantically. Kicking with all my might I swam towards her, my lungs tightening. When I crossed into the opening there was a whooshing noise and before I knew it, I was being sucked down a giant flume. Only not as fun as the ones at Rufflington Leisure Centre. I was now seriously short of breath and could hear a thumping in my temples. Princess whirled around in front like a sock in a washing machine. Then suddenly the atmosphere changed and my breath came bursting back. We clanged down on something metal, shaped like a funnel, and I gulped the air greedily. Another opening appeared below. Princess crawled towards it and looked up at me.

'You okay?'

I nodded. It was the second time in a week I'd nearly drowned with this girl.

'For someone called Anchovy you really are a

total wimp with water!'

She lowered herself in and I followed.

It was some kind of cockpit or control room,
covered in dials and levers, with two brown leather
chairs. Princess wiped herself with a towel, then
flung it at me.

'Where are we now?'

'You do ask a lot of questions, don't you? This is
the G.S.L. mini-sub. Try and keep up.'

She sat down, glanced into a periscope and

yanked a lever.

The contraption bubbled to life and I darted into the other seat. The area around the lever lit up into several small screens. One featured a purple dot bobbing along a web of lines.

'Is that dot supposed to be us?'

'Yep. We'll get you trained up on this, eventually. Have a look if you like.'

She swung the periscope at me. I squinted and peered through the glass. All I could make out was a series of stone vaults and brown, murky water.

'Are we in the sewers or something?'

'You got it. You don't want to go swimming in this. Hold tight.'

The sub lurched forward and downwards.

'Little waterfall there . . . Anyway,' she continued, 'a few years ago, the Trevi Fountain was granted a major renovation. Two million euros. Master Key pulled a few strings to get a mini-sub channel put in. This is the best way for us to travel.'

'We couldn't just take a bus again?'

'No, Anchovy. We can't take that risk. Big Alan Fresco will have his minions keeping an eye out in the city. Plus, you got a threatening note, ha!'

'That isn't funny.'

The water around us started gurgling more noisily. I looked into the periscope and saw the night sky framed by a stone arch. On the screen the purple dot was winding its way up a thick blue squiggle.

'This is the River Tiber.'

Strangely, I was beginning to relax. I enjoyed peering through the periscope, spinning it from side to side. I could see tugboats and jetties and sagging bridges up ahead. Gradually the scale of the buildings shrank and the shop lights grew less frequent.

I sensed we were following the river to the quieter outskirts.

I felt completely invisible to the outside world. I felt safe. I looked across at Princess, focused on the screen, her fingers flying over the controls.

'We're nearly there. Look out for a giant ice-cream cone.'

I saw the glow of a café or shop on the riverfront. There was a neon sign that read:

G-E-L-A-T-E-R-I-A—I-L—D-E-L-F-I-N-O

It had a logo of a flickering dolphin, and a giant plastic ice-cream cone in front.

'Here!'

We surfaced by a jetty, wriggled out of the hatch, and crept towards the ice-cream cone.

Princess leaned against it, knocked and chanted the motto from the G.S.L. banquet: *'Aureum in spatha est, vivat spatha!'*

There were three spheres of plastic ice cream in the giant cone – representing strawberry, chocolate and vanilla. They creaked and flapped open to reveal a face staring out. It was the Italian hacker boy from the G.S.L. conference feast.

'You remember Camillo, don't you?'

'*Buona sera*.' His voice was chirpy and nasal.

'Hi.'

'Climb in.'

'To the cone?'

'Yes, to the cone.'

These people had a thing about confined spaces. I got in, and Princess followed. Once again, it was like a funnel to a wider space below. Only the room it led to was much bigger than the mini-sub. It was a sort of laboratory. There were long workbenches, glass boxes, soldering irons, some computers and endless little drawers. These had labels on like 'X-ray glasses' or 'Parachute dressing gowns' or just 'Wafers'.

I saw that Camillo was dressed in a turquoise blue uniform with a sewn badge of the dolphin jumping over an ice-cream cone. I guessed that this was where the G.S.L. were stationing him.

'We are below the gelateria. Maybe you want some ice cream?'

'Hmmm . . . do you have pistachio?'

'We have everything.'

He disappeared up a flight of stairs. Princess turned to me.

'This will be the G.S.L. hub during Operation Stuffed Crust. It's a stone's throw from La Casa Bianca – where you'll be packing up the pizzas. Big Alan Fresco lives nearby.'

I gulped at the mention of Big Alan Fresco.

'Any trouble, report here. Camillo will be in most of the time. I'll be here sometimes –'

'– and *I'll* be here, too!' an annoying voice butted in. It was Justin, who had materialised out of nowhere. He was clutching a set of crayons, and I noticed a little table with some folded paper dolls, scissors and glue.

Camillo appeared with my ice cream.

'You stay out of trouble here, yes, Juice Box?'

Justin nodded. 'Can I have a raspberry ripple with hundreds and thousands?'

'You had one a minute ago!' snapped Princess. 'Can we get down to business, please?'

Camillo led me to one of the workbenches. His nose was running. I felt uneasy about the pistachio ice cream.

'So. Tonight we will give you the special equipment for your assignment.'

He strapped a watch onto my wrist. The face was shaped like a pizza and lifted up to reveal a screen.

'I like it.'

'This is the main way of communication, Anchovy. The phone will be hacked. You press here —' he dug his nail into the side '— and speak into the microphone, here.'

A menu came up on the screen.

'The important thing to remember is these two types of beep.'

He pressed a button and a low, staccato beep began.

'This beep is when anybody in the G.S.L. wants to contact you.'

He pressed another button. It made a different beep — high and constant.

'What's this for?'

'This is very important. It is the danger signal. If you hear this, get out of the area immediately.'

He turned it off.

'Maybe you have some questions?'

'No . . . well, not yet.'

He walked over to another workbench and picked up a can of black olives.

'I'm fine with just this ice cream, thanks.'

'This is not food.'

We walked over to a glass booth with a metal arm. It was a bit like those arcade games that claw for prizes but never pick anything up. Camillo opened a hatch and loaded the can into the arm.

He pressed another button and the arm flung the can against the side of the booth.

It burst open on impact and released a frenzy of black pellets, which bounced around wildly.

'Exploding olives. If you get in some trouble, you can throw these.'

'Okay.'

It was a lot to take in and the pistachio ice cream was melting everywhere. I took a lick out of politeness. Princess came over.

'You nearly done, Cam? We need to get Anchovy back to the hotel before sunrise.'

'Almost, Princess.' He picked up an L-shaped object with a small cylinder on top.

'That looks like a sort of gun.'

'*Si*, it *is* like a gun.'

'I don't want to kill anyone!'

'No, no, this will not kill anybody. Only burn, maybe blind, maybe they will have the memory loss.'

'I don't want to do that either!'

He ignored me and pointed to the small cylinder above the handle.

'Ammunition. In your case, you can try *sugo* – ah – the tomato sauce. Press here and it will go hot like a volcano into the eye of your attacker.'

Molten hot tomato purée?

'I really, really, really don't want to do that.'

'It was all in the contract, Anchovy,' cut in

Princess. 'Master Key has a laser ring. I like an old-fashioned poisoned dart myself.'

'I'm not using any guns.'

'It's just a precaution.' Princess sighed. 'Nothing bad is actually going to happen.'

And at that precise moment, as if they'd been waiting for it, someone turned off all the lights. In the darkness I was grabbed and shoved under the workbench. I heard a trampling of feet, a door slam open and some loud, gruff American accents.

I saw Camillo press a remote-control pad of some sort. Before I knew what was happening, the floor gave way and we dropped down to a tunnel beneath the laboratory. It was so shallow that we all just rolled right into it. Princess put a finger to her lips. The air became full with the sound of crashing and banging.

'No,' whispered Camillo. 'No, no, no.'

They were smashing up the laboratory. I heard

Camillo sniffle. His computers, his incubators, his robots. Princess turned to him.

'Shish kebab! I'm sorry, Cam, but we need to move out of here.'

'Princess, I want please to detonate the exploding olives.'

'In a sec, I promise.'

Princess then crawled ahead in the tunnel and we followed. We could hear the noise intensify above us, as whoever it was crashed over the tables and ripped up the floorboards.

'Okay, Cam. Do it.'

He must have hit the button on his pad that second. Instantly, we heard the exploding olives rattling around like a violent hailstorm.

'Aaaaaaaaaaargh, damn it!' came the cries from above. 'Move out, move out.'

We heard footsteps banging towards the exit. Then the words that no one wanted to hear.

'Raze it, Bruno.'

There was the sound of liquid sloshing around. Then a nasty smell.

'Petrol,' said Princess. 'Everybody out. NOW!'

We propelled ourselves forward on our bellies. Princess punched a flap in front of her and we saw the river, the hatch of the mini-sub peeking above the surface. Princess hauled me out and I stuck my legs through the hatch. I could see snotty tears streaming down Camillo's face.

'OMG,' I heard Princess gasp. 'No. No fluffing way.'

She was looking back towards the gelateria. Smoke and flames were billowing out from the shop front. Two shadowy figures emerged with a bundle under their arms. We ducked just in time. Princess slammed down the hatch and covered her face with her hands.

'They've got Justin.'

Chapter 9

y contrast, the hotel dorm was a picture of peace. Light arrowed through the shutters and gilded the boys' cheeks, nest-like hair and patches of drool. Even Dexter was quiet. *I used to be like them*, I thought. *Innocent.* I unzipped the ridiculous wetsuit and tumbled into bed. I felt sick with guilt. How had we forgotten about Justin? Yes, he was a pest. But wherever he was now, he was probably not having a very nice time. There definitely wouldn't be any raspberry ripple ice cream on tap. Shattered, I fell into a jittery sleep.

I was woken up by Hogstein himself.

'Get up this instant, Kingsley!'

I'd got so used to 'Anchovy' that I almost forgot my real name.

'Wuh?'

'The entire class is showered, dressed, breakfasted and sitting on the coach waiting for you! Do you know how selfish you are?'

'Sorry, sir.'

'Mark my words, Kingsley, your parents will be hearing about this. You have precisely one minute to get changed and onto that bus. GO!'

The coach was an echo chamber of jeers and insults.

'What d'ya do, Kingsley, wet the bed?' called Dexter.

Cue more laughs from the other snotheads.

'SILENNNNNNNNNCE!' screeched Miss Odedra.

Because I was last on the bus, I had to sit in the worst seat. At the front, next to crusty, musty, stinky old Hogstein. I remembered a history lesson where he told us that Queen Elizabeth I only had one bath a year. It seemed like he was following a similar course of personal hygiene.

'Isn't there any air-con?' I asked.

'What, Kingsley?' Hogstein shouted, his ears too full of hair to understand.

'Never mind.'

Rome was burning in the sun that morning. I looked out at the searing white marble, warped flagstones and bird-poo-spattered archways. Trams rattled past, graffitied in colours that popped and fizzed. A hundred scooters whined. Men in white shirts swore theatrically. A priest in a park bit into a watermelon and batted off flies. Eventually the driver slammed on the brakes and all the kids punched the seats, whooping like wild animals.

We saw a creamy curve of arches nibbled by the years.

'Children,' announced Hogstein, as if we needed it to be clarified, 'we have arrived at the Colosseum. Does anybody need to pee?'

Clad in our stupid bright-orange caps, we formed a line and trickled in like a high-vis caterpillar. I felt like I was in a giant cauldron with massive chunks missing. The floor stretched halfway across but had been sliced through to reveal a basement layer. There was also a pair of tour guides dressed as Roman centurions. I guessed they couldn't be wearing real metal armour, in this heat.

Hordes of tourists were pouring in. There were elderly German couples, American families, young men with big rucksacks, middle-aged Japanese women and many more. The Americans struck a pose with the centurions and took selfies. Most of them took photos before they even looked at anything. No one ever looks closely enough. Even if you're a member of the G.S.L. and you're trained to look, there's always one little thing you'll miss.

Hogstein stood in the middle of the gravel and raised his arms for attention. The sweat patches on his armpits were so big that they were practically meeting in the middle of his chest.

'Look around you, children. You stand in one of the most magnificent sites of the ancient world.'

'Where are the blood and guts, sir?'

'Not now, Dexter. Children – we shall split into two groups. Miss Odedra will take you lot . . .' He jiggled his bingo wings towards the hard-working girls at the front. 'And you lot . . .' *Please not me*, I thought. '. . . you come with me.' Of course.

The class dispersed and we followed Hogstein to the sliced-through basement.

Narrow tunnels ran left to right.

'Read your worksheets, children. Who can tell me what this part of the Colosseum was used for?'

'Was it the bogs, sir?'

'No, Dexter. Still, men probably would urinate here.'

Sniggers broke through the group.

'Where you're standing now is called the Hypogeum: the locker room. Write that down, boys. This is where the gladiators prepared themselves mentally. They'd sharpen their weapons, plan their strategy, say a few prayers –'

'And wet themselves!'

More sniggers from the idiots.

'You'd probably wet yourself, too, Dexter, if you were faced with certain death in front of thousands of people.'

We trooped up a level. The young men with backpacks had grabbed the fake swords off the centurions and were flapping them about. The centurions didn't seem impressed and stared past them. In fact, they were staring at us. Specifically, at me.

'Now children, here's a question. Why did the Romans kill Christians here?'

'For worshipping a different god, sir.'

'Excellent, Robin.'

Hogstein took out a ruler. 'So, when early Christians met, they used a secret code.'

With the ruler, he drew a big curve in the gravel.

'If the chap you were meeting was also Christian, he'd add another line.'

Hogstein added another curve. The two 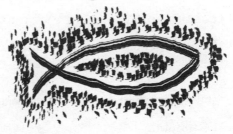 marks together made the shape above.

'The Christian fish. This was their badge of recognition. Fascinating, eh?'

Everyone stared at the ground. I thought of the anchovy I had tattooed on my toe. My own badge of recognition. I looked up and saw the centurions, still staring at me.

'Okay, everyone. Exercise three on the worksheet. Find an interesting feature in the Colosseum and do a little sketch in the box. Go off in pairs and come back in fifteen minutes. Any questions?'

Whether they understood or not, everyone shot off in different directions, eager to get away. Not wanting to be paired with Dexter, King of the Snotheads, I ducked back into the Hypogeum. It was quiet and cool there. I settled down on the bottom step and took out my pencil case. I looked at a little carving of some sort, but wasn't really taking it in.

My mind sort of glazed over and I was just about nodding off when a shrill noise cut through the air.

BEEEEEEEEEEEEEEEEEEEEEEEEEEEEEEEEEEP!

I froze.

BEEEEEEEEEEEEEEEEEEEEEEEEEEEEEEEEP!

There was no mistaking it. I looked at the watch Camillo had given me.

I flipped up the pizza-shaped face and saw a red dot flashing on the screen.

What had he said about the beeps?

BEEEEEEEEEEEEEEEEEEEEEEEEEEEEEEEEEEP!

A *flip-flap* noise came into my ears, mingling with the beep.

Camillo's words came back to me.

It is the danger signal. If you hear this, get out of the area immediately.

BEEEEEEEEEEEEEEEEEEEEEEEEEEEEEEEEEEEEP!

I dug my nail into the side button to silence the watch.

'Struggling there?'

It was a deep, gruff American accent. I looked up and saw a pair of tanned feet in sandals at the top of the steps. *Phew*, I thought. *Just one of the tourists.* Then the pair of sandals came down the stone steps towards me. *Flip-flap-flip-flap.* I looked up and saw my mistake. It wasn't a tourist. It was one of the centurions. He was carrying a spear, which I didn't remember from earlier. Before I could think why this was strange, the watch went off again.

BEEEEEEEEEEEEEEEEEEEEEEEEEEEEEEEP!

I looked down at the screen and saw text appearing:

Get out!!!

As I stood up, something whistled over my head and flattened me against the wall.

I opened my eyes and saw the stupid fluorescent cap. Only it was pinned to the wall by a quivering spear. At this point I didn't think. I just ran. I felt the centurion's plume as he went to rugby-tackle me. I felt my heel sink into his teeth one second;

the next, I was flying across the Hypogeum. I shot down one tunnel, turned left into another, then right into a smaller one. I could hear some tourists chattering in the distance. But where? A cloud of sand sprayed up around a corner. I saw the sandalled feet emerging and ran on. I heard the screaming whistle of the spear again. I've never run so fast in my life. In fact, if a Roman centurion with a spear chased me at school sports day, I'd be smashing gold medals every time.

'Get back here!'

As if I'd do that. I flung myself down a level, vaulting over scaffolding. I ran on, blindly – it all looked the same. Then I saw him again. A helmeted silhouette ahead, charging towards me. I realised it was the second centurion – they were attacking me from both sides! I was cooked – unless I could scale a nasty, knobbly old wall with nothing to grip. I scrambled upwards, my knuckles scraping against

the stone. Near the top was a cluster of scaffolding. I rolled onto it and looked through the gaps in the boards. I got a flash of the second centurion's armour, glittering harshly. He looked around. At that moment, when I was most scared – and, I'll admit it, very close to wetting myself – something ridiculous happened. A corny ringtone flitted across the Hypogeum. A tinny disco hit. It was coming from the centurion. He put the phone to his ear – blocked by a helmet, of course – and barked into it.

'Yo. You got him? . . . Sick, Bruno. Be right there.'

He hung up, spat into the sand, and marched off.

I lay on the scaffolding, my chest heaving. Bruno? The raid at the laboratory! The gruff American accents! Who were they? And why had they given up the chase?

My knuckles were bleeding. Hot tears began sloshing over my face. Hogstein. I had to find

Hogstein. As carefully as I could, I stuck my head out of the opening. I had come up in the seating at the north end of the Colosseum. I scanned around and saw the fluorescent orange of the kids' caps milling around the teachers. I'd never been so glad to see Hogstein. I hurtled towards them as fast as I could, my lungs almost bursting.

Hogstein spun around.

'Kingsley! What the hell are you playing at, boy? Late leaving the hotel, late leaving the Colosseum! You need to explain yourself this –'

'Arnold,' Miss Odedra cut in. 'Come on, Colin.' She could see I was upset.

I found Robin and we stood in line.

'All right, pal?' he said in his groggy voice. 'Want to see my sketch?'

'No.'

We made for the turnstiles.

I heard a pattering sound behind us.

Flip-flap-flip-flap.

'Excuse me, sir! Excuse me!'

It was the centurions. They had caught up with the group and were beaming away at Hogstein. I saw one handing him my orange cap. He spotted me and shouted: 'You forgot this, little buddy!'

I looked away. Hogstein bowed at them, then creased his pudding features into what might pass for a smile. He found me as we boarded the coach.

'What charming chaps. Excellent English, too. Didn't sound remotely Italian.'

He handed me the cap.

'Awfully nice of them, Kingsley. Lucky scrape that, eh?'

The coach pulled out and I glanced back. The centurions stood by the entrance, waving us off with a sickening grin.

'What did they say to you, sir?'

'They said they hoped to see us again soon.'

Chapter 10

o sooner had we driven a few blocks than I heard the horrible noise again.

Beep! Beep!

The sound of anything beeping gave me the sweats now. Thankfully this was just a text from my mum.

R u ok?

All fine, I wrote back. Except for nearly being speared to death on a UNESCO World Heritage Site.

Ok glad u r having fun love u lots precious darling sweetheart angel xxxxx

The world of Rufflington seemed like a
different planet to me now.

The world of Rome was difficult to take in
after that attempt on my life. After the Colosseum
we went to a few other places. We walked up a
giant flight of steps, which for some reason were
described as Spanish. We saw a lot of churches. We
saw a balcony belonging to a small, mean, bald guy
called Mussolini. And speaking of small, mean,
bald guys, we had to listen to a lot of Hogstein.

As we made our way up the hotel steps,
however, his mood lightened. Perhaps it was the
prospect of lasagne.

'You okay there, Kingsley?'

'Yes, sir.'

'Listen, Kingsley. I'm sorry I snapped at you. We
were just worried, that's all. You will let us know if
something's the matter, won't you, boy?'

His blotchy face took on a kindly glow.

'Yes, sir.'

'Good lad. See you at dinner?'

Beep-beep! Beep-beep!

This time it definitely was my watch.

'I'll see you later, sir.'

I hid behind a potted plant and flipped up the pizza face. Princess's face appeared on the screen.

'Anchovy, are you okay?'

'Yeah. I think so.'

'I can't believe how close that was earlier.'

'Were those centurions sent by Big Alan Fresco?'

'It's possible. I can't talk now, though. Go to the hotel kitchens at ten o'clock. Say the G.S.L. motto.'

The face dissolved into a dot on the screen.

Short and sweet, that was Princess. It must be stressful being a G.S.L. supervisor to an apprentice. Especially when there were stowaways and kidnappings and people getting spears chucked at their head. Once again, I thought of the two

centurions. Were they linked to the collaged note?
I dug it out and re-read it:

NeXt TIMe Youll Be Sleeping With The AnChoVies.

For some reason it felt familiar. I felt like I'd
been threatened with this note before. But surely
I'd remember something like that, wouldn't I?

Back in the dorm I had a quick wash and put on
some fresh clothes. In my wash bag I felt something
metallic and L-shaped. Camillo's molten purée 'gun'.

I hesitated, then tucked it into the trench coat.

'Coming to dinner, Colin?'

Robin had waddled over. He was a funny boy.
Quiet, slept a lot, but I liked him.

'Yep.'

The lasagne was warm and creamy and I wolfed
down an entire stick of garlic bread. The other

kids all seemed bright-eyed and cheery after our sightseeing in the sun.

I suppose they'd all had quite a different few days to me.

We'd just finished our tiramisu when Hogstein cleared his throat.

'I hope you enjoyed today, children. Tomorrow is an even bigger treat. Who can tell me what the Vatican is?'

'It's where the Pope lives, sir.'

'Sort of, Robin. It's the headquarters of the Roman Catholic Church. We will see the stunning St Peter's Basilica and the Sistine Chapel. What do you think of that?'

'Will there be a gift shop? My mum wants a fridge magnet.'

'Maybe, Annabel, maybe. Anyway – we expect an early start tomorrow, so it's lights out at nine o'clock!'

There was a groan of protest and a few boos.

'SILEENNNNNNNNNNCE!'

At ten o'clock I tiptoed down to the kitchen and knocked on the door.

'*Si?*'

I had to think of the G.S.L. motto for a minute before I got it.

'*Aureum in spatha est, vivat spatha.*'

Princess opened the door.

'This way, Anchovy.'

The kitchen was deserted, with the smell of bleach and a fly buzzing in the air.

I thought of my mum and dad's kitchen in Caesar Pizza after closing time. Princess led me out of the back door to a humungous wheelie bin.

'Get in.'

'What?'

'How many more times are you going to

question me when I ask you to get in something?'

'Well, you keep asking me to get in weird things.'

'Like what?'

'Like out-of-service buses and famous fountains and giant plastic ice-creams . . . and now wheelie bins.'

'This isn't a wheelie bin.'

She opened a little panel on the side of the bin. Which was strange, because normally you open the big lid at the top.

'Camillo built this. You'll like it.'

She crawled in, and I followed. It was becoming a bit of a habit.

'Whoaaaa.'

It was the nicest wheelie bin I'd ever been in. There was a shiny computer, softly glowing lamps, cushions, rugs, a mini-fridge – oh, and a steering wheel.

Perched at this were two familiar faces: the impressionist twins from the bowling alley.

'Hello, Anchovy.'

Once again, they were using my own voice to address me – and it was a bit creepy.

'You remember Yaconda and Yelena, Anchovy?'

'Hi.'

'You should be thanking these two from the bottom of your heart.' Princess brought out a glass bottle of pink lemonade and swigged it. 'They saved your life earlier.'

'We did,' the twins said in unison, now speaking in Princess's voice.

'Do you remember when those centurions were chasing you, Anchovy?' said Yelena, in a squeakier, entirely different voice.

It wasn't likely I'd forget.

'I remember one of them answered his phone because the other one said he'd caught me.'

'Right. We were monitoring all of that.' She turned what could have been an ignition key. 'In the blink of an eye,' continued Yaconda, now in a plummy sort of voice, 'Camillo hacked into their phones, got an audio file of their voices, and we did an impression of one of them to throw the other one off.'

'Er, it was just *me* who did the impression, Yack!' cut in Yelena.

'Whatever, Lena,' said Yaconda, now in a hoarse, gangstery voice. 'At least, *I* had the idea for it.'

'Well, it was amazing either way,' I said.

'Thank you, little buddy!' They were now imitating the centurion tour guide's voice – perfectly. I shuddered.

Princess laughed. 'We're heading to La Casa Bianca, Anchovy.'

'In this?'

'It's too risky taking the mini-sub two nights

running. Plus, that thing's a fluffer to charge. Inhales battery.'

Yelena yanked the gear stick and I felt the wheelie bin lurch forward.

'Hold tight,' said Princess. 'There's a seatbelt, which you should wear.'

'Hold tight!' said Yelena and Yaconda, in Princess's voice.

I fastened myself in and off we went, scudding along the cobbled lane.

The twins continued bickering.

'Oy, Lena, are you crazy? Third gear on cobbles?'

'Stop yakking, Yack! Big sis has this under *control*!'

'We're not exactly going to blend in with the traffic, are we?' I asked Princess.

'Anchovy – please. Obviously, we're going off road.'

The wheelie bin rattled madly over more cobbles. I was beginning to regret eating all that lasagne.

'These alleys run for blocks on end, each backing out from the cafés and restaurants. All G.S.L. affiliated.' She took another glug of pink lemonade. 'Which means they don't care if a motorised wheelie bin whizzes past their back door.'

'I feel sick.'

'Listen, kiddo, you need to feel better whether you like it or not. Tonight's the night.'

'Urgh . . .' I started swaying. 'What does that mean?'

'It means we're hitting Big Alan Fresco. Your first delivery.'

'You mean . . . I'm going *tonight*? To the guy who sent two centurion tour guides to kill me today?'

'Yes. And we don't know that for certain, Anchovy.'

'I think I'm going to vomit.'

Princess snorted. Yelena took off a cover from one of the cushions and thrust it under my chin.

'Be sick in this, Anchovy-boy.'

'If you have to,' added Yaconda, in a warbly robot voice.

I did have to. Horrible stinging chunks of pasta

and mince came raging out of my throat and nostrils. The cushion-cover sick bag plopped and swelled.

Yelena opened the hatch and flung the bag into an actual bin. One that wasn't speeding down the bumpiest road in existence.

'You know,' Yaconda said, now, oddly, speaking in Hogstein's voice, 'that the word "vomit" comes from the Latin word "*vomitorium*". This was a section of the Colosseum that forcibly discharged people.'

'I didn't see that on my worksheet.' I groaned.

Princess slung a bundle of clothes at me.

'You'll need to wear these.'

It was the uniform for La Casa Bianca, Big Alan Fresco's favourite pizzeria.

'The chef there is a crabby old lemon,' said Princess, 'so you won't have much chat.' She then did something very unexpected: she went and stuck her fingers in my ear.

'Urgh, what are you *doing*?!'

'Sheesh, Anchovy! I'm just giving you your earpiece!'

I felt a piece of plastic in my earhole, with distant voices tinkling away.

'I'm guessing that you're rubbish at Italian,' she continued, 'so Yelena and Yaconda here will give you some prompts. Camillo's on the line, too. Just repeat whatever they say.'

The twins gave me a thumbs-up.

'Remember,' said Princess, 'the police will let you in at Fresco's house when you show them the G.S.L. tattoo.'

Thankfully there wasn't much longer to go in that rattling vomit-box. When I staggered out and took a few gulps of air I began to feel better. Then I saw La Casa Bianca and felt sick all over again.

Chapter 11

t was a long, white building on the corner, with red and green frills above its glowing entrance. The people inside wore tuxedos or sleek black dresses and were dripping with jewellery. Some were nibbling pizza, while others huddled around a roulette wheel with counters and cards. This wasn't any old pizzeria – this was an *art thief's* pizzeria. A sour-looking whippet of a man in white overalls stood at a side door, smoking. I glimpsed his name tag – *Tomasi*.

The twins' voices crackled in my earpiece,

Say you're here for the job – '*Sono qui per il lavoro* . . .'

Which was followed by,

A bit basic, Yack.

I repeated the line, badly, and pointed to my La Casa Bianca uniform. Tomasi squashed his cigarette stub and thumbed over his shoulder. A blast of oily fumes hit me as we entered. I watched his knobbly back, twisting ahead through a warren of storerooms. He pummelled a set of swinging doors and we arrived in the main kitchen. My ears filled with the din of clanging metal, gas flames roaring, and the *rat-a-tat-tat* of a dozen chopping knives. Tomasi clicked his fingers, pointed to a tower of pizza boxes and growled, '*Guai a te se ti muovi e sta zitto!*'

Stand there and shut up, translated Yelena.

Kind of . . . quibbled Yaconda.

He grabbed a fistful of dough and thumped it

on the worktop. A muscle near his jaw twitched manically. He smothered the dough in *sugo*, flung some toppings on his beaten-up creation and slid it in the oven. Then he growled at me again and the twins translated:

If Signor Fresco doesn't like the pizza, you bring it back, understand?

I nodded. *Doesn't like it?* That seemed odd. I thought Fresco was addicted to pizza.

I opened up a box, feeling it was my cue.

Tomasi opened the oven, slapped the pizza in the box and brought his face level with mine. His cigarette breath was hot in my face. The twins paused. Camillo's voice chipped in:

You touch this pizza, bambino – Tomasi's bony fingers made a breaking gesture here – *and I'll kill you.*

He shoved me out of another door and pointed to a clapped-out bike. The road to Villa Campino spiralled uphill, into a darkness thick with the

sound of cicadas. My watch beeped with a message.

So far so good, Anchovy.

I pedalled through an avenue of olive trees and saw a red glow in the distance: police cars. It was the gatepost to Villa Campino, surrounded by officers. More sat in a control booth. I approached and a policewoman raised her spiky eyebrows.

'I'm here with Big Alan Fresco's pizza.'

She said nothing, then my watch beeped again.

Show the sign.

The sign! It didn't feel very slick, but I brought my foot up to the window, de-trainered, and whipped off my sock. I can't say it smelt of roses. The policewoman looked at the anchovy tattoo on my toe. She looked at me again. One of her spiky eyebrows flattened out. The other arched even higher. She took a deep breath, swivelled in her chair and signalled at the officers outside. The gates rumbled open and I was led towards the villa.

Its strawberry pink walls bristled with ivy like a badly shaven chin.

Inside, the pizza went through the same giant scanner you get in airports. Then a big door of a policeman strode up to me, all square shoulders and salt-and-pepper buzz cut.

'You the apprentice?'

I nodded.

'Captain Crudo,' he thundered, crunching my fingers in his blocky fist. 'We're also working on the search for *Girl with a Chipmunk*.'

'Don't you mean *Girl with a Squirrel*?'

He clapped a hand on my shoulder like a crane in a scrapyard.

'Listen, apprentice . . . whatever it's called, it's hidden somewhere in this house. The evidence is undeniable.'

He led me through a small, tiled antechamber with shelves of fluffy towels. A water cooler belched in the corner. There was a frosted glass door at the end, flanked by guards.

'Big Alan Fresco's private steam room. He never leaves the damn thing.'

Crudo rapped on the door.

'I hope you're ready for this, apprentice.'

Chapter 12

squinted through the mist to understand what I was seeing. It had all gone pear–shaped. I mean – he was actually shaped like a *giant pear*. All blobby at the bottom, with an oddly smooth, narrow top. I say 'oddly' – he almost didn't look real. And although he'd possibly sent two centurions to kill me, burnt down a laboratory and arranged the kidnap of a small child, part of me felt sorry for him.

'The pizza,' he wheezed.

I wiped my brow and crept towards him with the box. Through the steam, he reached out and grabbed it. I saw him open it up and pick at the toppings. For some reason I had expected him to gobble the pizza in a flash, not pick at it.

'So . . .' I stuttered, 'lots going on at your house, eh, Mr Fresco?'

He let out a long wheeze and ignored me.

I went in for the main topic of the day.

'Erm . . . are you familiar with the painting *Girl with a Squirrel*?'

There was a pause as he surveyed his pizza.

'I have seen girls. I have seen squirrels. But no paintings with such a title, little boy.'

I tried another approach.

'Do you like the artist Leonardo da Quincy?'

'B-list. I know little of him.'

I tried to recollect what I'd been told about this painting, in the document I flushed down the aeroplane toilet. I tried to picture that document like a film still, frozen in my visual memory. Then I had an idea.

'B-list?' I asked, trying to sound surprised. 'But I heard it's worth 20 million dollars.'

'Naturally.'

'Naturally? So you think that this artist is a nobody but is also worth 20 million smackers?'

He nibbled a slice of pepperoni – buying time.

'Would you say, from your vast experience, Mr Fresco, that it would be worth it to steal a painting that valuable?'

It was hard to tell if it was my question or just the steam room that was making him sweat.

'Fetch me a towel, you little brat.'

I was glad he wasn't going to the use the one wrapped around his elephantine waist.

I got him one and he mopped himself without a thank-you.

'I don't know why these police hunt me down . . . I am an artist! I have given beauty to so many!' He discarded a green pepper. 'And they want to punish me? Ask yourself, boy: what is the real crime against art?'

The steam was gathering in itchy beads of sweat. He was getting all deep and meaningful on me.

'You cannot answer that,' he puffed, 'because you are too young.'

'I'm just a pizza delivery boy, sir.'

I couldn't really see his face with all the steam, so what happened next was a surprise. He put down the pizza and roared with laughter. When his great hulk had stopped quivering he pushed the box at me.

'Take it away. I'm not hungry.'

He hadn't taken a single slice.

Crudo was kicking his heels in the antechamber. I wiped myself with a fluffy towel and downed a cup of icy water.

'What did he say?' he snarled.

'Erm . . . just that he was an artist, Captain. And that I was too young to understand.'

'Useless! To think that you're from the G.S.L.!'

He marched me back and out through security. My bike was still propped up by the control booth.

'*Arrivederci*, kid.'

I freewheeled down the hill, lapping up the breeze.

A spindly figure stood framed against the lights of La Casa Bianca. Tomasi.

I handed him the uneaten pizza in its box.

He just waved me away. I expected him to at least say something. But as I walked down the road, a nasty sound rang out across the car park. At first, I thought it was the croak of a demented bullfrog. Then I realised it was Tomasi – *laughing*. Something smelt fishy, and for once it wasn't an anchovy pizza.

Chapter 13

**EEEEEEEEEEEEEEEEEEEEEEEEEEE-
EEEEEEEEEEEEEEEEEEEP!**

There it was again: the danger beep. I
frantically scanned the crowd.

'How can you be so glued to that watch,
Kingsley?' barked Hogstein.

'Sorry, sir.'

BEEEEEEEEEEEEEEEEEEEEEEEEEEEEEEEEEP!

'Don't you have any respect, boy?!!'

I dug my nail in and silenced the alarm. We
were in the Sistine Chapel. All I could see was a
mass of tourists saying *ooh* and *aah* at the famous

painted ceiling. Very possibly, one of them wanted to kill me.

'You should be looking up,' whispered Hogstein, 'at one of the greatest artworks in the world.'

Up until now I had thought that Michelangelo was just my second-favourite Teenage Mutant Ninja Turtle (after Donatello, of course). But apparently, he was a pretty important painter.

'Just imagine, Kingsley – Michelangelo painted this lying on his back. Blinded as the paint dripped into his eyes!'

It *was* incredible. I couldn't even draw with a pencil sitting down for half an hour. This guy had painted a whopping great ceiling on his back.

A super-muscly Jesus was in the centre, with a whirl of naked bodies either flying up towards Him or down to a grimy-looking pit. People were getting prodded by pitchforks, dragged into flames, having their faces pulled about. It was like a giant

WWE wrestling match in the sky. There was even one bearded guy holding a big floppy bit of human skin. I couldn't stop staring at it. It was kind of like a onesie, or a fat suit without a person inside.

We left and traipsed across St Peter's Square. Guards in red-and-yellow jester suits with white fluffy bits on their heads stood with giant axes. I felt their eyes on us.

Then it began again.

BEEEEEEEEEEEEEEEE-EEEEEEEEEEEEEEEP!

I glanced back at the jester guards. The centurions again?

**BEEEEEEEEEEEEEEEEE-
EEEEEEEEEEEEEP!**

'Kingsley! I will confiscate
that blasted watch if you
persist!'

I silenced it. Miraculously, the
guards went off in the opposite direction.

We trundled up some marble steps into a
museum, and Hogstein went off on another waffle
tour.

The Uslizi Gallery, it was called. At least it had
soft leather seats. There were even some English
voices in one corner – a string of old ladies with
Zimmer frames and watercolour sets. They
reminded me of Rufflington and were, in a way,
quite comforting. It would have been nice to have
just sat back and zoned out. But actually, I had
work to do. G.S.L. work, I mean. I remembered
that the Uslizi Gallery is home to the painting, *Girl*

with a Squirrel. At least, *was* home. Before Big Alan
Fresco got his mitts on it. I went up to an attendant
with a mole on her eyelid and a stripy neckerchief.

'Excuse me, do you know where *Girl with a
Squirrel* used to hang?'

'Ah . . . this was stolen, little boy. I am sorry, we
do not have it.'

'I know, but where did it hang before?'

'Ah, it was not on the walls. They stole it from
the . . . how you say?'

She mimed a box-shape with her hands.

'Storage?'

'*Si*, storage. Very sad day. But we have many
other beautiful –'

'Thanks!' I said and darted off. I crept down to
the basement floor. There were signs for toilets,
boilers, janitor cupboards, fuse boxes and, at the
end, a set of doors that read *Archivio*. Archives.
It felt stupid not to have visited the crime scene

earlier. Captain Crudo had called the evidence 'undeniable', but I wasn't satisfied. Through the frosted glass, silhouettes shuttled back and forth. Obviously I couldn't just walk in. I couldn't be sure the anchovy tattoo would work either – coming here wasn't part of the plan.

I stepped back to avoid looking like I was loitering. Which I definitely was. I could hear the distant bark of Hogstein telling off Dexter, and the horsey laughs of the English grannies. I spotted a

painting titled *The Great Fire of Rome*. It showed a giant fireball swirling around, with tiny people in togas panicking. It gave me an idea.

I flipped open my pizza watch and dialled Camillo's number.

'*Pronto*, Anchovy! You are not with the school trip?'

'I am, but listen – can you do me a favour? Can you hack into the security system at the Uslizi Gallery?'

'Yes, it is easy, like a game for children.'

'Well, technically we are children.'

'What do you want me to do, Anchovy?'

'Set off a fire alarm and clear everyone out.'

'I understand.'

I heard his snot-crusted fingers dancing on a keypad.

'Do we need Princess's permission for this?'

'No, no, I don't think we need. But she will not be very happy.'

'I know. That's why I'm asking you.'

I saw his face break into a grin on the screen.

'Okay, Anchovy, it is ready. Anything else?'

It felt cheeky but I had to ask.

'Any chance we can make the CCTV drop for a few minutes?'

'Oooh, very bad, Anchovy. This will make trouble. But I like, ah, the *challenge*.'

I heard more tapping.

'You will get the blame for this, okay?'

'Of course, Camillo, thanks . . .'

Before I could finish, the air was cut with a harsh electronic wail. I hid behind a statue and held my breath. There was a babble of confused voices, then the intercom asked visitors to evacuate before a thousand shoes rumbled above me.

Eventually the stampede died down and a

message beeped on my screen.

Do not stay long. Fire services will come in 5 minutes – Camillo.

I slipped through the doors and gasped. I don't know what I'd imagined the storeroom to look like – but I wasn't prepared for this. I was on a circular landing that looped around a deep vault. Shelving was laid out in a sun shape, each shelf pointing from a circle in the centre.

I had a lot to answer for. I was going totally off-grid with the G.S.L.'s brief. I had rigged the security alarm of a major cultural institution. And I was bunking off from my school trip. Hogstein would go ape. All this and I had no idea what I was actually looking for. I just felt in my gut, or my heart – or wherever it is that instinct is made – that something in here would help me. But there were too many options. The shelves seemed to stretch on forever, groaning with bubble-wrapped artefacts, boxes and files. I only had four minutes to calculate which one contained information on *Girl with a Squirrel*.

I wandered down a line of shelves, hoping for some kind of alphabetical coding, but there was none. This was going to be a lot harder than Rufflington Library. But at the centre of the sun shape was my answer: a computer. Presumably the archive's catalogue. I messaged Camillo.

Can you hack me into the Uslizi catalogue system?

Ten seconds later the reply came back:

HACKED.

The screen flickered to life with a search box. I typed in 'girl with a squirrel' and a number of options came up. I clicked on the first heading:

THEFT.

This brought up the following information:

Title: Girl with a Squirrel

Artist: Leonardo da Quincy

Date: 1513

Date Acquired: 6/12/2014

Purchase History: click here

Police Report: click here

I hit 'Police Report'. I wanted to see just how 'undeniable' Captain Crudo's evidence really was.

Skim reading, I learnt this:

On 5 May, CCTV footage in the gallery went down. Police found an empty shelf where *Girl with a Squirrel* was stored, a bust back door and a drugged security guard. A witness reported an obese man leaving the premises with a briefcase. Soon after that, a stolen van was found on the road to Villa Campino.

The van was a three-seater and all three seats bore the impression of an extremely large bottom. From the side of the road, tyre marks like a tractor's led through the neighbouring olive grove. These led to Villa Campino, and therefore to Big Alan Fresco. The only possible culprit. He hadn't covered his tracks at all. It was all so easy for the police. Too easy, maybe?

Another message from Camillo beeped on my watch:

Firemen outside. LEAVE.

It was a valid point, which I should have listened to. But I was still curious. I clicked on the section 'Purchase History'. From this, I learnt that *Girl with a Squirrel* had once languished in some attic, suffering 'significant wear and tear'. Before entering storage in the gallery, it had been taken to an expert for repairs. I wrote her name on my hand:

Galina C. Forbes

None of this seemed out of the ordinary until I searched for her workshop online.

I wanted to interview her, but the only entry I found was:

'This business has now closed.'

Something stank. Before I could think what, my watch went off again:

BEEEEEEEEEEEEEEEEEEEEEEEEEEEEEEEEEP!

I looked up, expecting to see firemen coming in with a seething Hogstein. No one was there. But then I heard footsteps. Staggered footsteps, accompanied by a kind of scraping. I was about to hide when I saw the English grannies with their Zimmer frames. I relaxed – old people tend to like me, and they'd be pleased to see another British person who could help them to the exit. Perhaps this would earn me some brownie points with Hogstein, too.

'Hello?' I called. 'Are you lost? Can I help?'

They shuffled towards me, hunched over in their lilac peacoats.

'Thank you, dearie,' said the first one.

'Thanks, little buddy,' said the second.

I felt a cold trickle of sweat.

Little buddy. That wasn't an English accent. That was a deep, gruff American accent. And I knew where I'd heard it before. The grannies raised their heads, straightened their backs and puffed out their chests. They weren't grannies at all. They were the centurions.

My watch went into overdrive.

BEEEEEEEEEEEEEEEEEEEEEEEEEEEEEEEEEE-EEEEEEEEEEEEEEEEEEEEEEEEEEEEEEEP!

They removed their winged glasses and I saw their leering faces.

'We'd hoped to see you again.'

They were raising their Zimmer frames when an animal instinct told me to dive behind a shelf. I hadn't even hit the floor when the sound of machine guns rattled through the air. I hurtled down the aisle. Machine-gun Zimmer frames!

'Split!' I heard them shout. Shooting filled the air again and bits of artefacts exploded as they fired through the shelves. I ran and ran. A trolley was stationed at the end – carrying an enormous marble head. It was all that lay between me and the door, across an exposed stretch of floor. I burst towards it and as I did one of the grannies – or centurions – whatever – appeared around the corner. I shoved the trolley with all my strength. It crashed into the granny and spun madly, the machine-gun Zimmer frame clattering to the floor. The trolley spun again and saved my life a second time: from the other direction granny two was approaching. The marble head absorbed a spray of bullets. I lunged for the door, rolled down a ramp and was in a car park. Then I sprinted towards the fire engine, school bus, kids and a raging Hogstein.

'What is the meaning of this, Kingsley?!!!'

I'd never seen him so purple.

'Unacceptable! Never in all my years of teaching have I –'

'Sir, sir!' cut in Robin. 'Those grannies are waving at us!'

The firemen were leading out the grannies, who miraculously had become stooped over again.

'Thank you, dearie,' one of them called to me. 'Until next time.'

Robin looked at me and started laughing.

'Colin, your cap!'

He stuck his finger through a hole in the peak. 'Ha! Looks kinda like a bullet hole!'

Hogstein barged him aside.

'KINGSLEEEY!' he bellowed. 'I demand an explanation. NOW!'

Chapter 14

'We've looked for him everywhere!' shouted Princess. 'Delegates in every café, bakery and ristorante, turning Rome upside down to find that damn Juice Box. Nothing!'

Master Key frowned on our watch screens. 'This is really not ideal.'

'Of course it's not ideal!' Princess scowled. 'But then again, *someone* let Juice Box travel in their fluffing suitcase when he should NEVER have been here!'

She gave me the Skewer-stare.

'Yes,' brooded Master Key. 'That was

disappointing, Anchovy. You need to be far more vigilant.'

I sagged with embarrassment.

'This mission has been a disaster,' continued Princess. 'Stowaways, arson, assassination attempts! Plus, you think it's cool to set off a fire alarm in a pretty public location. And on top of all that, a kidnapping! Why you allowed –'

'Actually,' I snapped, 'we *all* took our eye off Justin – not just me!'

'I'll look into it,' purred Master Key. 'Anchovy,' he said in a kindlier tone, 'I want you to look at these faces.'

Two mug shots appeared on my watch screen. I recognised the leering grins of the centurion-grannies.

'Know these two?' asked Master Key.

'I'll be having nightmares about them for a while, yes.'

'Brutus and Bruno. Fresco's cronies. He must be in touch with them, somehow.'

I shuddered.

'Things need to pick up fast, Anchovy. But I believe in you. Meeting adjourned.'

His face dissolved on the screen.

'It's a miracle Master Key even managed to get you into La Casa Bianca.' Princess sighed. 'But then, he's Master Key.'

A dreamy look came over her. Damn Master Key, the smoothie.

I wanted to tell her about this '*Galina C. Forbes*' I'd written on my hand. Something about that woman's name was bothering me, but I couldn't think what.

As the gelateria had been burnt to a cinder, we had a new meeting spot. It wasn't the most spacious: the old lift in my hotel. One of those gilded-cage types that would've had a bellboy

pushing buttons. Camillo had rigged it to stop on the attic floor. The twins had imitated an engineer on the phone; nobody would be coming to fix it any time soon. Princess opened the top, conveniently placed beneath a hatch in the roof of the hotel.

'Give me a foothold.'

I cupped my hands and she shoved her foot on them, almost kneeing me in the face.

I felt her hands on my shoulders as she pressed close.

'Don't even think about it, Anchovy. I'm a full two years older than you.'

Cue the beetroot face. She bunged open the hatch, swung herself up and reached down for me.

I gripped her calloused hands and she hoisted me up. We perched on the roof and the breeze fanned our faces. I thought of the night we biked up to Buckdean Hall, with all of Rufflington below. Now we had all of Rome before us.

All its wonky rooftops and bell towers and domes. I squinted at the Palatine Hill in the distance, the Tiber snaking below. Somewhere down there lurked Big Alan Fresco.

'Camillo should be here soon to take you to La Casa Bianca.'

'How are we getting there?'

'Helicopter, he tells me. Here he is!'

'That's a helicopter?'

What you might mistake for a rusty robotic bat was approaching the rooftops. It was more a hang-glider than a helicopter. It did at least have a big propeller that Camillo had nicked from somewhere, as well as a gearbox cluttered with buttons. He landed the thing on the roof and a few tiles slid off.

'*Ciao*, Anchovy. Climb on board.'

'To that thing?'

'It is a very good machine. Only crashed one time.'

Princess reached into her backpack.

'Put this on. Your parents would disapprove otherwise.'

It was a bike helmet. Not something that would save me if I plummeted to the streets.

'You did sign a contract, Anchovy.'

By now, I was beginning to get used to this. And I was thinking less of it.

There were two saddles like on a tandem bike, with Camillo in front.

'Princess, can you make a push?'

She pushed with all the aggression I'd expect, and we sped along the rooftop.

I grimaced as the air whipped my cheeks – then a big nothingness opened below.

'Pedal!' Camillo shouted in his nasal yap.

My legs went into overdrive. I closed my eyes. But the ground that would splat us never came. We were flying. I tried not to look down at the pulsing maze of factories and motorways. Camillo didn't bat an eyelid. Obviously, he had flown homemade helicopters before.

'I am happy this was not in the fire,' he muttered, giving the rickety frame a pat. His voice seemed to fade out, as if behind thick glass.

'It was three years to build our laboratory . . .' He rubbed something from his eye, pretending it was a midge or a gnat or something.

'I'm sorry, Camillo,' I said. 'If you tell me what to do, I'll help rebuild it with you . . .'

I meant it, though as my DT teacher would verify, I'm shocking at building things.

'*Grazie*, Anchovy. Well, I have seen my machines destroyed before. I remember, before the G.S.L., there was this sub-aquatic quad bike that I was making . . .'

'Coooool.'

'Yes . . . it had a little camera to record all the fishes. I made it a very beautiful green with an orange frame . . .' His eyes gleamed, like a proud parent. 'It was at the boarding school. When the other boys were sleeping, I was making the sub-aquatic quad bike.'

'How long did it take?'

'Oh, maybe six months, something like this.'

He veered left and we buffeted on a thermal.

'If I speak honestly, I made it to escape from the school. I was going to ride home along the bottom of the river. I do not know how the other boys found it.'

'What happened?'

'Well . . . ah . . .' He pretended that pesky midge got in his eye again.

'They were idiots, Camillo.'

'Yes. This is true. I am lucky that Master Key found me.'

I squeezed his shoulder. That's what my dad does if I've had a bad day at school, which is a lot.

'What's Master Key's story?' I asked. 'I mean, why is he so . . . distant?'

Camillo shrugged.

'This is complicated.'

He filled me in. Apparently, Master Key had been boss for three years – the maximum number for a G.S.L. president. He had a family of English aristocrats on one side, Japanese chefs on the other. But something had happened. Something bad. No one knows what exactly, only that Master Key had lost all contact with his family. This seemed standard for the G.S.L. Princess had used her forgery skills to convince her parents that she was at military school, and her military school that she was home-schooled. The twins never even knew their parents.

As we approached the outskirts, Camillo drew us closer to the buildings.

I recognised the gelateria by the giant ice-cream cone, reduced to a charred shell. I saw the land surrounding Villa Campino, lush with cypress trees stabbing the sky. Here I remembered the report from the archive, and scoured for the obvious clues that the police had lapped up. The stolen van was still outside, surrounded in police tape. Then something else caught my eye. It can't have lasted more than a second: the flash of a figure, sprinting across the olive grove.

Chapter 15

omasi was in his usual place, marked by the red dot of his cigarette. His silhouette resembled some of the wire sculptures in the Uslizi Gallery. I followed him again into the bowels of the restaurant and watched him pummel another pizza for me to deliver. He remained silent, didn't even ask me how my day was. I pretended to go and fetch some boxes for him in the store cupboard. I was determined to load the purée gun this time. I found a tube and fixed it in the holder.

Setting off with the delivery, I waited until I was

out of sight then fired at a tree trunk. The molten tomato powered out like a laser. A plume of smoke rose, revealing a neat hole, as if drilled in. I felt reassured that it actually worked but didn't feel any more confident about using it on someone. Even if they did have machine-gun Zimmer frames.

The climb up to Villa Campino was just as gruelling as the day before and the policewoman in the security booth was just as moody. I peeled off my sock again to show the fading anchovy tattoo. She pinched her nose, raised her spiky eyebrows and waved me in.

After security I met Captain Crudo, grinding his teeth.

'We still can't find that damned *Girl with a Stoat*.' He scowled.

It's a squirrel, I wanted to shout.

Police were swarming all over the place, searching for this pesky picture. The rooms had been emptied, the walls were bashed in and the floorboards ripped up. What remained of the furniture looked like it had been chewed up by a pack of hungry dinosaurs. Even a beautiful piano had been taken to bits, its lid against a wall, the strings in a sad tangle on the floor. How hard could it be? I've struggled to find my pen lid sometimes, but surely a painting was a bit harder to hide.

We strode into the antechamber and knocked on the door.

'You better have some sharper ideas this time, apprentice.'

The steam this time seemed even hotter and thicker. I took a big gulp of water and approached the pear-shaped silhouette of Big Alan Fresco.

'You again . . .' he rasped, glistening with sweat.

'Here's your pizza, Mr Fresco.'

He opened the box and began plucking off the toppings.

'Tomasi is a genius,' he mumbled through a mouthful of red onion.

'Do you know him well?'

'I've known Tomasi a long time, young man. Since before you were even born.'

I was noticing his Milton Keynes accent more now, creeping through the fake Italian one. I mopped my soaking forehead with my T-shirt and looked again at the writing on my palm. The name Galina C. Forbes was starting to smudge. It was still bothering me.

'How do you feel about having all these police in your house, Mr Fresco?'

He paused as he played with some olives.

'I feel invaded, of course. They are searching for that wretched painting, I hear. Why, I don't know . . .'

'They want to know who swiped it off the gallery walls, that's why.'

'The gallery walls? Not the walls . . .' he began, then stopped himself.

'You're right, Mr Fresco, it wasn't taken off the walls,' I continued. 'It was taken from storage. Which you knew.'

He curled his lip in disgust.

'I am not used to being spoken to like this by a mere pizza delivery boy.'

'And I am not used to being shot at by grannies and centurions, Mr Fresco.'

'Not my problem . . .' he wheezed.

'So you admit that you sent them?'

'How can I do anything that you accuse me of, little boy?' He brought a fluffy towel to his face. 'I am unable to leave my house. And unless you bring me bad pizza, I have no reason to want to kill you.'

He hurled the towel into a corner. For the first time, I was able to see him up close through the steam. He was surprisingly handsome; dark chiselled features, topped by a sculpted mop of hair. He handed me the box.

'Take it away. I don't want any more.'

Crudo stood with his arms crossed as I left.

'Anything to report?'

'Er, no, Captain . . .'

'Useless!'

Tomasi took the pizza box and waved me away as though he was swatting a fly.

As I left the kitchens, I saw a message from Princess:

Guess what I just found?

Chapter 16

e stood around the ruined shell.

'Frankly, Crudo,' said Princess, 'I knew you wouldn't comb the grounds properly.'

It turned out that Fresco had hidden the painting under an abandoned farmhouse, concealed by weeds at the edge of the Campino grounds.

'We already looked here, young lady,' snapped Crudo. 'How would I know to pull this lever disguised as an old brick to reveal a secret storage chamber below?'

'You wouldn't,' said Princess, rolling her eyes.

'That's why your government got the G.S.L. involved. We see this kind of thing, like, all the time.'

On releasing the brick-lever, a large dome of weeds lifted up, and a hatch and ladder appeared. We climbed down into the bunker, which was neatly kitted out like a nice little holiday home. A bed, sofa and kitchenette took up one half, tables and chairs the other. On the table were a glass of milk, half a brownie, a TV guide and an abandoned game of Scrabble. And lying there on the Formica worktop was da Quincy's masterpiece, *Girl with a Squirrel.*

So this was what all the hype was about.

It was smaller than I expected, about the size of a dinner tray. For some reason I was disappointed. This was worth 20 million? Worth arson, kidnapping and attempted assassination? Then I peered closer at the girl in the painting. The softness of her features placed her at about thirteen, fourteen – only a few years older than me.

But her snooty stare, with the head tilted back and one hand on her hip, made her seem older. Her eyes were oddly spaced apart, one with a droopy lid. A lock of auburn hair tumbled out from a dark green headband. I could see the grease on her bony nose, the purple-turquoise veins in her temple and the stray hairs between her eyebrows. And the squirrel! I could see the saliva on its tooth and the twitchiness in its eyes. I could practically feel its reddy-brown fur and its little heart smacking against its ribs. I got the sense that at any minute, it would leap from the girl's clasp and run away. In short, I could see everything. It was breath-taking. I thought back to the possessed corgi picture at Major Marjorie's. This was in a different galaxy of skill, let alone planet.

'Well, children,' boomed Crudo, after shoving the brownie down his gullet, 'you may have accidentally found the bunker – but ultimately I was right: *Girl with a Weasel* was right here, on the grounds of Villa Campino! Simple!' He banged his anvil-fist on the table and sent the Scrabble board flying.

'Firstly, Crudo,' said Princess, 'it's a squirrel. Secondly, you just ate a piece of evidence. Thirdly, *nothing* in this world is simple.'

I wiped my brow, unable to take the heat in the kitchenette.

'A bunker-beneath-a-farmhouse job?' Princess continued. 'Don't you think that's just a little too . . . textbook?'

Crudo nursed a smear of brownie on his tight white shirt. He was on the ropes.

I pictured a mental film still of the dodgy police report again.

'The tyre marks through the olive grove,' I chipped in. 'The giant buttock marks in the stolen van's seat. It's like he *wanted* us to find it!'

Princess grinned. *Bossing it,* she mouthed.

'You think this is all FAKE, little boy?' scoffed Crudo.

I looked at my hand and saw the smudgy words '*Galina C. Forbes*' again. My eyes fell on the Scrabble pieces and my head began to spin. Of course! I grabbed a handful of the letters and spelt out:

'Look!' I switched the letters around:

GALINA C FORBES

BIG ALAN FRESCO

'Stop playing games, child!' called Crudo. 'I

have important police evidence to gather.' He went
to grab the painting.

'Wait!' Princess blocked him and pressed her
watch. 'I'm getting Master Key on the line.'

Master Key's soft voice filled the bunker.

'Good afternoon, team. Do we have a new lead?'

I took a deep breath and shared my thoughts.

'According to the archives in the Uslizi Gallery,
Girl with a Squirrel had been 'restored' by a woman
called Galina C. Forbes. Don't you see? Galina C.
Forbes *is* Big Alan Fresco!'

'Hmmmmm,' purred Master Key.

'And isn't he a known art forger?' I continued.
'He must have swapped the painting for a fake,
surely!'

Crudo grabbed the painting and began
marching towards the ladder.

'Oh, this is just childish nonsense!' he chided.
'He's not made a fake painting and he's not

deliberately got himself arrested! This painting is now police property!'

'Xavier,' said Master Key. 'That painting is going nowhere until it undergoes extensive authenticity checks.'

'But Master Key —' spluttered Crudo.

'Xavier. You know Interpol's position on this. The buck stops with me. End of discussion.'

Crudo pulled a face like he'd been sprayed with cold sick. He tossed the painting on the table and flounced off.

'Well played, Anchovy!' said Master Key.

'You're learning fast.' Princess smiled. She opened the bin to chuck in her chewing gum. 'Whoa!'

She plucked out a string of folded paper dolls, then flipped them around. On the reverse side, scrawled in clumsy crayon, were the words:

DOWN WITH THE G.S.L.!!!

A new mental film still came to me: the same paper dolls from Camillo's laboratory, before the raid.

'This is bad . . .' groaned Princess.

'What do you mean?' said Master Key.

'I mean', said Princess in a quivering voice, 'that we have a mole. A horrible, nasty little mole who's been telling Fresco everything.'

Everything seemed to go silent as it dawned on me. The little figure in the olive grove. I could barely get the words out of my dried-up throat.

'Justin.'

Chapter 17

'Look alive, Kingsley!' I felt the force of the packet explode in my face, the liquid blinding me.

'Dexter!' scolded Miss Odedra. 'Did you just throw your milk carton at Colin?'

'It sort of fell out of my hand, Miss, honest. Kingsley's face was in the way.'

I dried my face with a napkin and gave him the evil eye. We were having breakfast in the hotel. I had been sleeping nicely until Dexter's missile.

'What's all this?' fussed Hogstein.

'Kingsley's spilt his milk, sir!' Dexter whined,

then bit into a pastrami sandwich.

He gave a yelp.

'M-m-mustard! This sandwich has got m-m-mustard in it and I'm allergic!'

At that moment the waitress dropped the bill onto my table and slunk off.

When I realised it wasn't a bill at all and was addressed to 'Anchovy', I unfolded it and read:

We need to talk about Justin.
P.S.

She was in the bin area. I could tell it was Princess, even with her back turned and a different hairstyle.

I took my tray over and scraped my plate into the bin next to her.

'Don't look at me, Anchovy,' she muttered.

I looked back at the tables. Hogstein was trying to perform a Heimlich manoeuvre on Dexter. He seemed to be coping okay.

'Did you put that mustard in Dexter's sandwich?'

'Maybe. He's a pain in the bee-hind, isn't he?'

'Yeah. But he's no Justin.'

'Correct. Camillo ran a DNA test on that collaged death threat you got. Justin's dirty prints are all over it.'

I was running out of morsels to scrape so I picked up someone else's plate and scraped that. I pictured Justin making the collages and another mental film still came to me.

'Of course,' I said, 'the scissors and paper dolls.'

'Yeah. He was making that note at Camillo's laboratory. I was right there!'

'Why did he do it?'

'It's hard to know.' She slammed some crockery into a bucket of soapy water. 'But when you met on the beach, that was like an audition for *both* of you.'

'What do you mean?

'I mean that there was only one position for the apprenticeship. You got it.' She balled up her rubber gloves and flung them into a bin. 'And basically, he kind of hates your guts.'

'Thanks.'

'We'll deal with that little fluff-weasel later. What's more important is that Fresco is communicating to his network. We need to find out how.'

She wheeled the trolley to the kitchens and slipped out of sight.

I went back to my classmates. Dexter was breathing normally again and Hogstein was addressing the group. I saw that his tie was spattered in meatball sauce.

'Well, children, today is our last day in Rome! Are you sad?'

No response. He pointed outside.

'Okay, team! To the Historymobile!'

We took him to mean the bus. Once everyone was on board, he rattled off the usual.

'Our next stop will be the Baths of Caracalla. Exciting, eh?'

Still no response.

'Ancient Romans took their baths very seriously, children. They even had them all together – hundreds at a time!'

'Urgh! That's sooooooo not okay!' shrieked Annabel.

'Could everyone see each other's naughty parts, sir?' shouted Dexter.

'If they had eyes and actually found that interesting, then yes, Dexter.' Hogstein sighed. 'But they weren't just baths. They used to also contain shops, sports fields, hair salons, music pavilions, museums.'

It's worth emphasising the words 'used to' here. When we piled off the boiling coach, all we saw

were crumbly walls, gappy arches and sunken pits.

'Where's all the water, sir?' shouted Dexter.

'It's an ancient site, Dexter,' groaned Hogstein. 'Now – I want you to answer all the questions on your worksheet –' he looked at me '– and stick to your buddy at all times.'

Robin tugged at my sleeve. I let out a huge sigh of dread and off we went.

I couldn't stop thinking about Justin's betrayal. Why would you betray the G.S.L.? I'll admit they had their flaws. All those confined spaces being one. Never really sleeping was another. But overall, they were my friends. They didn't throw milk in my face anyway.

The sun beat down, searing the kids' freckles from pea-size to sprout-size. Dexter found an old bit of pillar and began writing 'Rufflington Rovers FC' in marker pen on it, until he got screamed at by Odedra. The gardens around the site had been scorched yellow, the ground all hard and bumpy. I sat on a cool slab of marble and watched a line of ants. They were marching over cracks that must have seemed like ravines to them. They formed a production line, passing little leaves, the husk of a nut, fragments of olive. They were right at home in this Ancient Roman site – a well-drilled troop of builders and marchers. When I was feeling the sun on my eyelids and drifting off to the drone of cicadas, Robin's voice broke the spell.

'Coliiiiiiiiiiiiiiiin!'

'What?'

'Come and look at this mosaic!'

'How about *you* look at the mosaic and I stay here?'

'Mr Hogstein said we should stick together at all times!'

How did Robin have so much of a conscience?

'Okaaaaay . . .'

The mosaic was laid into a sunken recess flanked with olive trees. Although sections were missing, we could make out the scene: a wild battle between gladiators. And even though it was just little square stones, we could see so much detail: the mace swinging around one guy's head; the torn strap of a sandal; the worried eyebrows of someone about to get pulped. I recognised that feeling – I'd been experiencing it a lot this week.

'Shall I read the worksheet questions out loud, Colin?'

'In your head is fine.'

No sooner had we sharpened our pencils than the Michelin-man shadow of Hogstein blackened our view.

'Mighty impressive, eh, boys?'

'Yes, sir,' cooed Robin. 'Very impressive.'

It was impressive, but Hogstein didn't need flattering like that.

'Mosaics: wonderful what ancient man could do. Pushing little coloured objects around a surface to tell a story.'

I kept my attention on the worksheet, which I was struggling my way through. One section needed a diagram and I asked Hogstein for a ruler.

'Certainly, Kingsley. Good to see you knuckling down.'

He fished in his satchel and handed me the ruler. When I tried to use it, flecks of sand spread across my sheet. I blew them away and remembered: Hogstein had used this ruler to draw a line in the sand in the Colosseum. The marking that early Christians had used as a secret symbol. And then, like a punch in the chops, the answer hit me. Symbols. Lines. Big Alan Fresco was using a secret code. Hogstein's line about mosaics now rang in my head:

Pushing little coloured objects around a surface to tell a story.

It was simple: the pizza toppings! Fresco was arranging them to write some sort of message! Which meant that the person delivering the messages was the same person trying to stop them: me.

'GOT IT!!!' I shouted, throwing my clipboard and pencil into the air. I began dancing around like an idiot. 'Got it! Got it! Got it!' Fancy Hogstein giving me the idea! I don't know what got into me, but I actually hugged the old fluffer! He went a sort of burnt strawberry colour.

'Now, now, Kingsley. I am glad you've, er, found this mosaic so . . . exciting.' He tugged at his tie. 'But please don't throw your clipboard around a World Heritage Site like that.' He tramped off to check on the others.

'What was that about?' asked Robin.

'Never mind.'

★

'Colin,' cried Princess when I told her. 'That's incredible!'

I felt the classic beetroot cloud spread over my cheeks. She wasn't supposed to call me by my real name.

'You mean "Anchovy",' I whispered.

'Master Key will be loving this.' Her eyes gleamed. 'An apprentice busting Big Alan Fresco on his first outing!'

'We still need to work out what the messages actually mean, though.'

'Obvs, Anchovy.'

We were taking the mini-sub to La Casa Bianca. Princess wanted to 'mix it up', in case anyone was watching the skies for Camillo's helicopter.

I thought back to the last time we'd used the mini-sub, after jumping into the Trevi Fountain. She a caterer detective superstar, me a nervous nobody. Things felt different now.

'I've done some research. There's a sewage canal that takes us right into the grounds of Villa Campino.' A map appeared on a screen in the cockpit. The grounds of Villa Campino sort of resembled a bow-tie shape. She touched an area in the south-west of it.

'We'll surface and drop you off here, near La Casa Bianca. When you get out it might be a bit . . . well, pooey.'

There went the romance, then.

I passed the journey with my eye on the periscope, watching the sliding shoreline of collapsed stone walls, sewage pipes and dead cats. Eventually more tree branches clawed their way into the picture, and I sensed we were nearing the Campino estate.

'Remember,' said Princess, levering the sub upwards, 'don't tell Fresco what you know about the pizza code.'

'I won't.'

'Seriously – there could be an almighty reaction if he knows we know.'

I changed into my La Casa Bianca uniform. We surfaced in a small pond in a playpark.

'La Casa Bianca is a few minutes that way. Keep me posted.' She shut the hatch and the sub sank below. As I walked towards the restaurant, I thought about Tomasi. He was the point of communication, the one receiving the pizza messages. I typed into my watch:

P.S.: P.S. just realised – someone should tail Tomasi from now on. Anchovy.

On it. Will send the twins. P.S., Princess replied.

Tomasi greeted me with his usual twisted face. It was like he was constantly biting into a mega-sour jelly sweet.

As he led me through the narrow passages, I spun my head around, taking mental snapshots of every detail. What I was hoping for was an open desk drawer, an unlocked office or, better still, a wall chart illustrating the pizza code. But surely it couldn't be as easy as that.

Tomasi saw me looking and biffed my hat off. People seemed to like doing that.

He returned to work, chucking flour about. I winced each time he pounded the dough – he seemed angrier than usual tonight. When he began to lay out the toppings I paid closer attention. Now his words on the first day made even more sense:

You touch this pizza, bambino, and I'll kill you.

Chapter 18

downed a cup of iced water and entered the hell chamber.

It seemed to be even more roasting than usual. Fresco was dripping – no – *gushing* with sweat. I tiptoed closer and wiped my forehead.

'How are we today, Mr Fresco?'

'Fine, boy.' He wheezed and took the pizza box. 'Actually, I'm not fine. I've been feeling the strain of this investigation . . .' He nibbled an artichoke. 'This blot on my reputation.'

It seemed to me his reputation was well blotted before this house arrest.

'Are you feeling ill, Mr Fresco?'

He rubbed his droopy mega-moobs.

'My heart. It aches. Never have I been so wrongfully accused in all my days.'

'I'm sorry to hear that, Mr Fresco.'

I watched him at work with the toppings. It was obvious now – there was a design to all this picking. He held a mushroom between his finger and thumb, reviewing his next move like a master chessman. He placed it on the edge of the crust and looked at me. 'Anyway, I understand you won't be with us for much longer.'

I gulped and hid my face in the cup of water. How did he know I would be leaving? Or did he mean something more threatening? I wouldn't have put it past him.

He waited for an answer, but I couldn't think of anything. We just stood there, watching each other in the steam.

'Get me a towel,' he finally wheezed. I
handed it to him and he dabbed himself daintily.
'Remember, little boy, who you are dealing with.
Think about that on your little bunk bed tonight.'
He closed the pizza box and thrust it at me.

'Get out of my sight.'

Outside, I opened the box and took a mental
snapshot of the pizza. The toppings didn't exactly
form letters, but they were definitely laid out in a
design. Slipping it into the satchel, I found myself
handling it more delicately than before, like it was a
work of art.

Tomasi could tell. He caught me watching him
open the box.

'*Esci da qui!!*' he spat, his cigarette flying at me
like a bullet. I didn't need the twins' translation to
know he meant *get outta here!!*

I walked away from La Casa Bianca, looking
over my shoulder. When I saw Tomasi disappear

into the kitchens I knew I had to act. I had to know what he was doing with those messages laid out in toppings. I scuttled back to the door and listened to his footsteps fading. I rounded each corner with caution until I saw him. He was locking up the main kitchen and cursing. In his other hand he held it: the coded pizza. I snuck into a cleaner's cupboard, covered myself in aprons and left the door ajar. His steel-capped boots clicked past, then clattered down some steps. I counted to ten, then followed.

I arrived at a loading bay and bin area packed with pallets. Across the forecourt and through a maze of girders, I saw a strange light spilling from a battered door. As I approached, I heard Tomasi muttering – almost chanting.

If he caught me now, I'd be done for. I reached inside the trench coat and took out the purée gun. With my eye against the keyhole, it took a while to process the scene: Tomasi was crouching on the floor, praying. All around him were icons, statuettes of saints and flickering candles. There was even an altar and crucifix. It was a chapel, concealed in the storerooms of La Casa Bianca.

I spotted the pizza box, open on the floor. Next to it was a small Bible and a waiter's pad and pencil. Was this just Tomasi, taking some time after work to spiritually reflect? Then I looked again and

realised he wasn't praying. He was opening up
the Bible but the pages didn't move. Instead, there
was a hollowed-out compartment, from which he
removed a tiny book. It can't have been bigger than
a train ticket.

He spun around to look at the pizza. Then he
looked at the tiny book. Then he wrote something
down on the waiter's pad. He repeated this again:
looking at the pizza, looking at the tiny book,
writing something down. I realised that it must be
a breakdown of the toppings – a codebook. I had
to have it. As I adjusted my angle, my cap brushed
against the handle of the door. It was the lightest
contact, but enough to make a rattle. Tomasi
looked up and charged towards the door. He flung
it open and his eyes bulged in rage. I dived away as
his arm lashed out.

'You little worm!' he spat in English. 'I will
break you! I will destroy you, little boy!'

I flew through the kitchens, out to the car park and jumped onto my bike like a seasoned Hollywood stuntman. I turned for a second to see Tomasi's spidery limbs propelling towards me, before pedalling with all my might back towards the mini-sub.

I explained Tomasi's ritual to Princess. I told her about the little chapel in the loading bay, and the Bible where he hid the codebook. I also told her Tomasi had caught me spying. She groaned at this last part but smiled.

'Great work, Anchovy,' she said. 'I mean – almost great work. Getting caught looking through a keyhole . . . so rookie.'

'I *am* a rookie.'

'I know. But you're doing the hard stuff well, just stop fluffing up the basics!'

Black velvety water, probably sewage, sludged

past us outside. The flickering dials cast pink and yellow outlines on Princess's face.

'We need that codebook badly,' I said. 'It's the only way to read the messages.'

She looked across at me, bags forming under her eyes.

'I'll come back to you on that in the morning, Anchovy.'

'It is morning,' I groaned, looking at my watch. 'Two a.m.'

We surfaced below the Trevi Fountain and slipped on our wetsuits, which was tricky in that shoebox of a cockpit. We kept bumping into each other and chuckling nervously.

A homeless man on a bench was the only person to see us wade out of the fountain, but he was too tired to care. As we flopped back into the hotel car park, I was picturing only one thing: bed. I would probably need to sleep for a whole month once I got back to Rufflington. *I really should text my parents*, I thought. I was beginning to write a message when my watch started beeping like crazy.

BEEEEEEEEEEEEEEEEEEEEEEEEEEEEEEEEEEEP!

Princess grabbed me by the shoulders and threw me beneath a box hedge.

'Get down and shut up!' she hissed. 'And turn off your fluffing watch!'

We lay there motionless. Princess peered through the leaves. I followed her gaze towards the school coach, parked and ready for our drive to the airport. Except it wasn't going anywhere. Two burly men stood guarding it with knives in their hands.

I didn't need a granny or centurion outfit to recognise them.

Chapter 19

rutus grinned at Bruno. Bruno nodded back. Then they marched towards the box hedge. I gripped the soil and stared at Princess.

The gun, she mouthed. But it wasn't there. It was in my trench coat, which was in the mini-sub. And I was lying in a flowerbed at two in the morning wearing a wetsuit. Through the gap I saw their feet. Not in centurion sandals or granny clogs but big, mean man-boots. *So this is it*, I thought. *My life is over*. And it had been going so well. I looked back at Princess. Was this the last image I would ever see? My G.S.L. supervisor face-down in the mud? The thuds grew louder and a shadow swallowed us up. My heartbeat was deafening. I looked up, expecting a henchman. But there was nothing. And then the strangest thing happened. Instead of getting louder, the thuds grew quieter. They were actually walking *away* from us.

What the fluff? mouthed Princess.

We watched them leave the car park, then crept to the hotel.

'Be careful, Anchovy,' said Princess when we parted on the stairs. 'They've probably trashed your room.'

I expected slashed pillows, feathers in the air, furniture in bits. Maybe they'd tied up Dexter.

'Just stay out of trouble on your last day. We'll pick you up after lights out, as per.'

I tiptoed into the dorm to survey the carnage. But it was the usual peaceful scene of snoring boys and Robin burbling something about 'teddy'. Somehow I took off my wetsuit and sank beneath the covers.

A measly three hours later, I was woken by a voice crashing into my eardrum.

'THIS IS THE LIMIT, KINGSLEY! YOU HAVE REALLY GONE AND BLOWN IT NOW!'

The boys stood around my bunk, stunned, as Hogstein took centre stage. He was screaming his lungs out.

'THIS IS THE END OF YOUR TRIP, KINGSLEY! THE END OF YOUR TIME IN THIS SCHOOL! THE END OF EVERYTHING!'

His glasses were steaming up, his sausage fingers were gnarled and his big beefy head seemed to swell with rage.

'W– wuh – what have I done, sir?' I stammered,
tears welling in my eyes.

'DONE? DONE?' He bared his teeth at me.
'Kingsley, you insolent wretch!' He held up a spray
can. 'I found this under your bed, young man, so
don't try to fool me!'

He then yanked me out of bed and frogmarched
me down the stairs. Miss Odedra and the other kids
followed. His voice trembled as we passed through
the lobby and out of the hotel.

'Kingsley, I am SO disappointed in you . . .'
He led me to the bus and I still didn't get it. 'After
yesterday, at the mosaic, I thought we were seeing
eye to eye.'

I thought back to my moment of madness when
I'd actually *hugged* Hogstein.

'But this morning, we found this . . .' He waved
his hand at the coach.

My heart sank. I realised now what Bruno and

Brutus had been doing. The tyres of the coach were slashed. And on the coach itself, spray-painted in red, were the words:

HOGSTEIN STINKS OF EGGY FARTS

I was too shocked to find it funny. (Which it was, in isolation.) All I could do was blurt out the classic: 'It wasn't me, sir!!'

'Don't give me that rot, Kingsley! Spray paint beneath your bed and the hotel manager says he saw you in the car park earlier. With the chambermaid, I should add.'

There were a few muffled snorts of laughter here.

'But sir – check the CCTV! I didn't do it!'

'Who else would do this? Eh?'

I bit my lip. Two gangsters working for an art thief? Saying the truth would have made Hogstein even madder.

'And by the way, Kingsley: I do *not* smell of eggy —'

He was interrupted by the wail of a police car. It pulled up next to the bus and a policeman in sunglasses jumped out. He examined the graffiti, fussing and clucking like a wet turkey.

'Shocking, officer, I know,' bumbled Hogstein. 'But I assure you the lad in question will be —'

The policeman lurched over and prodded me.

'Little boy,' he announced, 'you are under arrest.'

The other kids gasped. Odedra yelped. Hogstein flapped.

'Now really, officer, I don't think this is necessary . . .'

The policemen prodded him now.

'You too.'

We were too stunned to clock that we were being handcuffed and shoved into an Italian police car. Being squashed in with Hogstein felt like sharing a seat with a snorting bull. One that had just been dumped at a red-themed disco. He protested more, but the policeman and his colleague didn't listen.

When we pulled up at the station, they whipped off their sunglasses and gave me a sickening grin. I should have seen it coming.

'So nice to see you again, little buddy.'

Chapter 20

hey left Hogstein in a waiting room and threw me into a booth. No windows, no furniture. Just a wall of filing cabinets and a knackered fan. Hands behind their backs, they edged towards me.

'Whaddya reckon, Brutus? Taser gun this time? Or maybe get the Alsatian in?'

Their big ugly man-boots crunched a little closer.

'Or just the good ol' fashioned police truncheon?'

I scanned the room for an air vent to jump

through. Or a loose floorboard to wriggle under. Or even just a chair to throw at them.

'Heh-heh. You put up a tough ol' fight, little buddy.'

They raised their truncheons.

I crashed into the filing cabinets and closed my eyes. I heard the *DOOOOM* of truncheon against metal. The *KRRRRRR* of my T-shirt ripping. The *PHTTTTT* of a pizza detective flying up against some drawers. And the *CLAAAAANG* of that same pizza detective being dragged *inside* a filing cabinet. I say filing cabinet; it was clearly a big metal box that had been faked to look like one. And I hadn't been dragged in there by Brutus and Bruno. I found myself staring into the big dark eyes and flaring nostrils of Princess Skewer. Which was strangely nice, but also painfully awkward.

'What the . . . ?' I spluttered. 'Where . . . ? How . . . ?'

'Not the fluffing time!' She hit a switch and the filing cabinet began to rotate.

Yes, rotate. When it turned around 180 degrees it spat us out into a kitchen on the other side of the wall. We could hear the *bang-bang-bang* of bad cop and badder cop smashing up the place next door.

'Was that a . . . ?'

'Revolving filing cabinet, yes.' She dusted herself down. 'What did you expect, a revolving bookcase? This isn't the 1930s, Anchovy!'

I looked around. We were flanked by bread trolleys as the scent of cinnamon wafted through the air.

'Is this a G.S.L. place?'

'Yep. Handy being close to a police station.'

Suddenly there was a crashing of pots and pans and trays and vats.

'Shish kebab! This way!' she shouted, and we tore through a storeroom and out the back door.

We could hear Bruno and Brutus clattering through the kitchen.

'Outta my way! Move! Move!'

As we flew across the bin area the back door crashed open. They burst out, covered with flour and jam. Pelted by Italian G.S.L. delegates, I guessed.

'Run, Anchovy!' yelled Princess.

We sprinted towards a wheelie bin – *the* wheelie bin, I hoped – and clambered through the hatch. The twins were at the wheel, arguing over who was going to drive. As soon as we got inside, the whole contraption began to judder. Brutus and Bruno were banging the fluff out of it on the other side.

'You're going down, little buddy! Down to Chinatown!!'

'So lame . . .' Yelena sighed and hit the controls. We zipped off, but instead of heading *out* along the alleyway we were going around in a circle.

'What are you doing, Lena?' Yaconda moaned.

'Stop yakking, Yack – big sis needs to concentrate!'

On the control panel, the word 'MAGNETISE' appeared in glowing orange letters. Then an image of the bin area came up. As the flour-and-jam-spattered maniacs ran around, our wheelie bin seemed to be backing into *other* wheelie bins. I half wondered if the twins had lost the plot, when I noticed that the other bins were joining onto ours – magnetically. We rattled to and fro, joining them up until we had formed a train of wheelie bins.

'Here's the fun part,' chuckled Yelena. She circled the bins around Brutus and Bruno, like wagons in a cowboy film.

'Do you want to do the honours?' Yaconda pointed to a green button.

The words 'TIP OVER' had come up on the screen. I hit the button. In one deadly motion, the

circle of wheelie bins – all except ours – opened
their hatches and rocked onto their sides, showering
Bruno and Brutus in every kind of muck you could
imagine.

'Aaaaaargghhh!'

Bin bags split and gushed all over them: potato
peel, fish bones, crusty old cans, half-finished
takeaways and gallons of grease.

We zoomed off, laughing.

'Good work, team!' shouted Princess. 'To La
Casa Bianca!'

'Are we getting the codebook?' I asked.

'*I'm* getting the codebook, Anchovy. Right now,
we can't have any more fluff-ups. No offence, but
you *are* still an apprentice.'

She handled me a bundle: the trench coat and
purée gun, which I'd forgotten in the mini-sub.

I had a good long sulk until we pulled up at La
Casa Bianca.

'You can watch and learn from this, Anchovy,'
she called in a patronising tone.

She and the twins discussed the plan: hack
Tomasi's phone, pretend to be Fresco, tell him the
G.S.L. were coming and that he should chuck the
codebook into the nearest wheelie bin (ours). A
nice ruse, but I didn't feel like buttering them up.
But when Yaconda dialled, the line went dead.
Apparently even the G.S.L. had problems with
signal. They tried a dozen times, sighing and
groaning and fretting and tutting. Yelena kept
saying that 'big sis' had it under control. Big sis
didn't. They didn't bother asking if I could help. *No
offence, but you are still an apprentice.* After a while, I'd
had enough. I threw on the trench coat, puffed out
my cheeks and climbed out.

'What the fluff are you doing?' hissed Princess.

'I've got this,' I said in my best action-hero
voice. 'Where are the exploding olives?'

Chapter 21

omasi was by the door, puffing out smoke like a chimney in a strop. His bloodshot eyeballs slid back and forth. Then he slunk back into the chapel. I ducked behind the crates and saw a message on my watch:

You must pull the rings off to activate the cans. Be careful. Camillo.

Since the exploding cans were effectively grenades, he had a point.

There must have been about two hundred of them on the pallet. I slowly drew them out and snapped off the rings. Then I began to restack them in a tower on a large plastic tray. It sounds weird, but I felt like a toddler with building blocks – carefully balancing them on top of each other, hoping no one knocked them over. And like a toddler, I was totally absorbed. All that mattered was stacking these cans. If I got it wrong, it could result in some serious olive injuries. Eventually, the cans were tall enough to hide my head when I held the tray.

This is it, I thought. I pictured the headlines if it all fluffed up: *Death by olives: schoolboy tragedy in Italian loading bay.* I hefted up the cans, slunk out from behind the pallet and walked as calmly as I could across the forecourt. I could only see from the waist down and could just make out the metal steps that led to Tomasi's lair. I climbed them slowly, taking extra care. But one rung was slippery and I missed my step. For a second, the explosive tower wobbled dangerously. I closed my eyes and took a deep breath.

Focus, Colin. Somehow I steadied myself and made it to the top step. And then I realised the one major flaw in my plan. The door. How could anyone holding two dozen cans of explosive olives also knock on a door? I couldn't wait here forever.

Just as I felt all circulation go dead in my arms, I heard a voice. A deep, gruff American voice.

'Hey, Tomasi! Open the door, will ya? Got a little surprise out here!'

If I had been close to wetting myself in the Colosseum, now I was pretty much 99.9999999 per cent there. I waited for the truncheon or the spear or the Alsatian or whatever it was to charge at me from behind. But then, the sweet, sweet realisation: it was the twins! They were speaking from my watch, imitating Bruno and Brutus!

The door creaked open. Tomasi grunted at what he saw: a strange wobbly tower of canned olives with a pair of legs beneath it. *This is it,* I thought. *We need that codebook.* His spider arms reached towards me. Sweat trickled in my palms and my legs began to shake. He was falling for it. He thought this was a delivery. I handed him the tray and, in that second, he saw my face. He croaked in alarm, staggered with the weight and, finally, as I brushed past him, he toppled into the loading bay with twenty-four cans of exploding olives. There was a deafening *BOOOOOOOOOM*. Gas billowed out and black pellets bounced around madly, banging off the girders and smashing the windows. Entering the chapel, I replayed the mental film still from my last visit.

By the altar, the lectern. On the lectern, the Bible. Inside the Bible – the codebook. On the well-thumbed cover was the title:

The Dough Vinci Code

I tucked it into my pocket. Tomasi was writhing on the tarmac as the olives nipped him like mosquitoes on steroids. 'NOOOOOOOOOOOO!' he moaned.

I now saw the second major flaw in my plan. How do you cross a loading bay in a storm of exploding olives? My answer came in the *DONK* of a dustbin lid, hurled against the doorframe and very nearly taking my head off.

'Use it as a shield!' called Princess, who had come out of the wheelie bin and chucked it from somewhere. 'Cover your head and run, come on!! You can do it, Anchovy!'

I held it up like a gladiator and legged it, not without the pesky olives giving me a few nips in the ankle. We stumbled into the wheelie bin and they all began cheering:

'Anchovyyyyyyyyy! Anchovyyyyyyyyy!'

I laughed and thanked the twins for their impression of Brutus and Bruno.

'You're welcome, little buddy,' said Yelena, still in character. 'I thought that would do the job.'

'What are you on about, Lena?' said Yaconda, also in character. 'It was *my* idea.'

'Oh, stop yakking, Yack!' I tried joking.

'Hey! Leave my little sister alone!' shouted Yelena.

'Will everyone get out of their nappies for a second?' yelled Princess. 'We've got Fresco on the ropes! And I emphasise the word "we" there, kids.'

She was right. It was the best I'd felt all week: Fresco was writing in pizza toppings, as I'd guessed. Inside the tiny book was page after page of diagrams of pizza slices with differently arranged toppings. Underneath each arrangement was a letter of the alphabet. There was even a system for numbers, too. Best of all, it included a chart explaining to Tomasi how to read the pizza toppings:

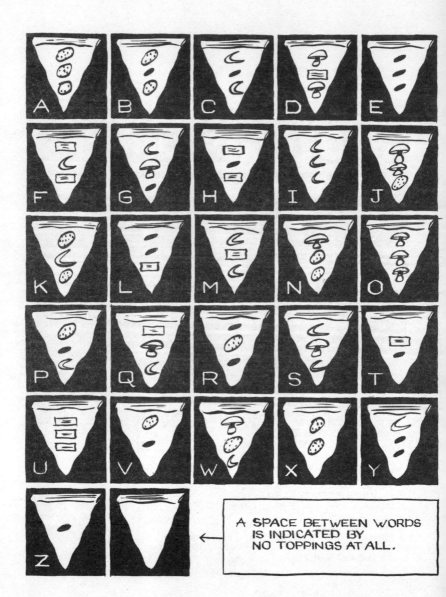

A SPACE BETWEEN WORDS IS INDICATED BY NO TOPPINGS AT ALL.

I mean, it was a pretty odd way to message your cronies.

Then again, Fresco *was* pretty odd. And he did have a lot of time on his hands.

'Yelena, step on it: we're heading to Villa Campino to tackle Fresco square on,' said Princess. Yelena revved up the wheelie bin, 'Anchovy – can you remember the toppings he sent back to Tomasi?'

I paused.

'Can you lend me some pencils and paper?'

I thought back to what Master Key said to me when we first met:

Your memory. You have an extraordinary gift.

Princess brought me pencils, paper and a pink lemonade. I closed my eyes and tried to think of all the pictures that were in my head. I lined them up like film stills. Then I got myself back to my first visit to Fresco. How was the pizza when he handed it back?

I searched my memory and found the footage.
It was like rewinding a film. Finally, I pressed
the mental pause button of me
looking at the pizza. Quickly,
I tried to draw it, to capture
the way the pizza toppings
were arranged. It looked
like this:

I repeated this process for my
second visit to Fresco. The
pizza looked like this:

Then for the third
evening:

I tore all three sheets out of the pad. With Princess's gum we stuck them to the wheelie bin walls, what with there being zero floor space. Then I studied the codebook. I went back and forth, through all the pages, all the options. In some cases I remembered, through the mist of the steam room, Fresco's fingers making the shapes. Funny how none of them involved anchovies. He hated anchovies. We were just winding our way up the hill to Villa Campino when I had the message scrawled down. And to say it was cryptic would be an understatement.

This is what the toppings spelt out:

RFF1 CUT OPEN THE FISH 8LT.

I showed it to Princess.

'What the fluff? Cut open the fish?'

'I know.'

'I don't get it.' She sighed. 'I thought that would

be the answer – a location of some kind, something that told Tomasi what the plan was.'

We pulled up by the gates.

'We'll grill him on these messages and find out where that painting is stashed.'

'Okay.'

'Seriously – this is our last chance.'

We parted from the twins and climbed out. As Princess and I approached the security booth, a horrible thought crossed my mind.

'Princess, I don't want to sound like I'm giving up . . . but what if Fresco doesn't actually know where the painting is?'

'I don't like your attitude, Anchovy,' she snapped. 'Fresco knows. We need to know. And we need to know now.'

Outside the villa, there were more police cars than usual – as well as ambulances. Our watches started beeping with an urgent red glow. A face appeared on our watch screens: Master Key. He closed his eyes and took a deep breath.

'I hope you're ready for this, you two.'

We stopped in our tracks. His silky voice had a trembling quality to it.

'Big Alan Fresco is dead.'

Chapter 22

hey had thrown a white sheet over his great hulk, giving it the appearance of an iceberg. No one had thought to turn off the steam, which still shrouded the room.

Crudo was talking to the medics and wiping himself with a towel.

'As far as I'm concerned,' he boomed, 'that's case closed. We found *Girl with a Gerbil* in his house. And Fresco,' he gestured to the corpse, 'had a heart attack when he found out. Simple.'

'Captain,' said Princess, '*Girl with a SQUIRREL* is a fake. And nothing in this world is simple.'

'You kids just like to complicate things. Take him away!' he snapped to the medics.

'Wait!' I had spotted something peeking out from under the sheet. Before I could think why, I threw it back.

'What are you doing, apprentice?' shouted Crudo.

There was an opening in the floor, partially covered by Fresco's beanbag-sized buttocks.

'Urgh, Anchovy! You sicko!' Princess cried. 'That's his toilet!'

'He never left this room, kids. He had to go *some*where,' said Crudo, shaking his blocky head.

'You mean he just sat on his toilet non-stop? That's rough!' said Princess, covering her mouth.

Fresco's body was even more saggy than usual. It was like a deflated hot-air balloon, and his head had sunk into his chest. Some weird instinct made me grab it and push it back. The medics gasped,

Crudo swore and Princess screamed. Because what we were looking at wasn't Fresco's head at all. There was no face – just a gaping hole. I got another film still in my head: the weird piece of floppy skin in the painting in the Sistine Chapel. *It was kind of like a onesie,* I had thought. *Or a fat suit without a person inside.*

'Someone help me flip this thing over!' I called.

We rolled over the body and there it was, almost invisible in the mist of the steam room: a zip, an actual zip, running down Fresco's back.

I had the feeling I was in a science lesson, dissecting a frog or a pig's heart.

'Anchovy – what are you . . . ?' Princess gasped.

I grabbed the zip and pulled. There was a farty wheeze as the deflated body fell apart. It was empty.

'It's a fat suit!' I shouted. 'Fresco isn't dead! He's escaped!'

I shone my watch light into the toilet. A set of rungs led down into darkness.

'Down the toilet?' moaned Princess, in a pre-puking kind of voice.

It seemed dodgy, but I had to spell it out.

'He crawled out of his own fake bottom, yes.'

'Urrrrrrrrrrrrrrrrgh!'

'Call for back-up!' Crudo barked to the guards outside, then he turned to me. 'What are you implying, apprentice?'

I took a deep breath.

'Firstly, Captain, my name's Mark Anchovy. Secondly, it's obvious, isn't it?' I gestured to the fat suit. 'Fresco ate nothing but the odd pizza topping. He was sweating buckets in this steam room. He shrank in size and left via the toilet!'

I went over to the escape tunnel and peered in. It was now or never.

'I'm going in.'

The room fell silent, except for the whirring of the steam machine. Princess was the first to speak.

'I'm coming with you, Anchovy. I am your supervisor, remember.'

Crudo shrank back and tugged on his tie.

'I'll, erm . . . stay here and check there's no trouble.'

'Whatever.' Princess shrugged. 'I'm copying in Master Key.'

She typed a message. We took a deep breath of whatever fresh air was left and clambered into Fresco's toilet. The stink was like a slap in the face. Even his turds were violent. We had no idea how far ahead he was, or when he had left. But we had to go after him. The ladder kept on going down, deep underground. We bounced around ideas as we climbed.

'The fake painting makes sense now, Anchovy, I get it.'

'He faked his death to close the case, you mean.'

'Yep. Crudo nearly did close it as well. Painting retrieved, criminal dead.'

'But why did he even need to fake-steal the fake painting if he'd already got the real one?'

'Because he wanted to mess with our minds. Like all master criminals . . .' She patted me on the shoulder. 'Only he didn't reckon with you being a sicko who looks in people's toilets!'

I grinned and shone my torch ahead. The shaft finally ended and a tunnel began to level off. There was no sign of Fresco. Just the sound of our footsteps echoing against the rock. Princess got out her poisoned darts. I took out the purée gun. It was cramped and dark and we upped the tempo, eager to find the end. After about ten minutes a pinprick of light bobbed up ahead. It was the opening of a cave, carved out in the sunrise like the last white shred of a hardboiled egg. And then we saw him. Fresco – but not as we knew him. He had transformed into a small, skinny being. He looked almost boyish. But I recognised the handsome features and sculpted coif that had struck me on my last delivery. He dipped out of sight and we crept to the cave's edge. Crouching behind a boulder, we saw a rocky beach with a jetty. Fresco climbed into a speedboat, flanked by Brutus and Bruno in dark suits. In the front seat was our betrayer – Justin. He smirked up at Fresco.

'Dirty little fluff-sack,' muttered Princess, giving him the Skewer-stare. Perhaps Justin sensed it. Or perhaps, by some fluke, he happened to look at the space above the boulder. Either way, he saw Princess's ponytail and recognised its twisting shape. In a second, he was bawling like a baby.

'GET THEM!' Fresco roared.

Brutus and Bruno sprang across the rocks, reaching into their pockets. Princess unleashed a

blow-dart at Bruno, which lodged in his stomach.
I pointed the purée gun. My finger was on the
trigger when my cap flew off and the rock behind
me exploded. I heard a scream and saw Brutus
clutch his hand, his gun clattering into a rock pool.
A hole had been burnt through his suit, and molten
tomato – or blood – was smeared all over his hand.
I got up to run but was pinned to the ground by
Bruno, snarling in my ear like a wild animal. He
brought up a rock but dropped it, as Princess sank
her teeth into his wrist. His other hand whipped
my face and knocked me off my feet. I was dimly
aware of Princess screaming, of Fresco laughing
and Justin cheering. There was a split second as
I hovered in the air before all became water and
darkness. It was the second time in a week that I
had been submerged in the sea. The bubbles roared
in my ears. The speedboat blared off. I couldn't see
seaweed, or rocks, or the bottom of any seabed. Just

a deep bluey-blackness. Something long and slimy wrapped around my ankles.

I sensed the wriggling and scuttling of sea creatures. *Cut open the fish.* It hit me now. The fish. The anchovy. Me. What Fresco meant was simple: kill Colin. Open me up.

I closed my eyes and saw a jerky swarm of images. I saw my dad mopping the tiles in Caesar Pizza. My mum's freckled hands tucking down my collar. Alicia, twanging on her double bass. G-pops, whistling to Dinnergloves. I would never see them again.

Chapter 23

linding light surrounded me. A white
tunic swam before my eyes. Clouds
unfurled in the distance. I felt weightless.

'Anchovy? Anchovy? Can you hear me?'

A slim face with multicoloured eyes looked into
mine.

'Master Key?'

He let out a long sigh. I felt his hand on my
shoulder.

'He's alive, Princess.'

She darted into the room and threw her arms
around me. She had a bandage around her head,

which gave her the appearance of a mean tennis player.

'Don't squash him!' said Master Key.

I tried to sit up and coughed up salty water. I could hear the drone of a motor and glimpsed a cockpit through a small door.

'We're on a seaplane, Anchovy. Belongs to a monster yacht I was working on undercover.' He patted a steward's uniform, then swapped it for a patterned dressing gown.

'I headed for the shore when I got Princess's message. I just grabbed your ankles when you went under.'

'What happened to you?' I asked Princess.

She wiped her eyes.

'After Bruno chucked you in, they went for me. I hit my head but ran into the tunnel and lost them, the fluffers.'

Master Key went into the cockpit.

'We're tracking Fresco now,' he called. 'He caught a chopper out of Italy.'

Princess handed me a cup of hot chocolate. I took a swig and its warming creaminess burbled into me.

'Where is he now?'

'Over France – we're making up ground,' said Master Key and sipped his perfume-y tea. 'Also, Yelena and Yaconda reported that Tomasi left yesterday. He boarded a UK flight.'

'So we've got our work cut out,' added Princess.

I glanced around the cabin and saw my mum's trench coat hanging above a little heater, the pockets emptied. The purée gun rested on a seat, while my papers had been stretched out on a ledge to dry. I noticed I was dressed in Master Key's pyjamas – a golden yellow silk with a red trim, the diamond of spatulas stitched into the breast pocket, above the initials M.K.

'What about my school trip?' I asked feebly.

Master Key laughed. 'You've nearly died and you're thinking about that?'

'I just . . . I'll probably be expelled now.'

'Listen, it's fine. I'll put the twins on loudspeaker and they can fill you in.'

Their voices – whatever their real voices were (I still didn't know) – crackled into the cabin.

'Anchovy! You made it! Here's what Yelena and I did –'

'*I* want to explain, Yack! Anchovy – we phoned your teacher, Mr Hogface.'

I didn't bother correcting her.

'I pretended to be you, telling him that the police had escorted you to the airport, as they didn't want you to miss your flight.'

'Yeah – he went a bit ape at that,' continued Yelena, 'but *I* smoothed it over, thankfully. I phoned as your head teacher back in Rufflington.

We told Mr Hoghead that all was fine, and that he should meet you at the airport –'

'And *I* had the idea to then phone the police station,' cut in Yaconda, 'pretending to be the hotel manager. I told Mr Hogfeatures that there had been a mix-up and that they had arrested the wrong boy.'

I wish I had these twins' superpowers, I thought.

'Then it got a bit interesting,' said Yaconda.

'Our hardest assignment yet, I reckon, Yack,' said Yelena. 'When he got to the airport, we had to phone Mr Hogwash as your other teacher, Miss Odedra. We said that she was already on the plane with you, and that he had to sit at the back as there were no seats nearby.'

'Oi, don't forget, Lena,' said Yaconda, 'we also did Mr Hogbreath's voice *to* Miss Odedra, telling her that *he* had Anchovy with him.'

'I didn't forget, you interrupted, Yack,' said

Yelena. 'Anyway – this way none of them knew that you weren't there. We also had some G.S.L. cabin crew who chucked a few sedatives in their lunch. So they didn't get out of their seats.'

My head was spinning.

'And to cut a long story short, Master Key pulled a few strings at the airport. He got the staff to hurry them through, delay Mr Hogstains in Customs, and no one had a clue.'

'*Plus*,' finished Yelena, 'we phoned both teachers as your parents, saying all was well.'

Master Key, Princess and I broke into a round of applause. Was there nothing they couldn't wangle?

'Also, we'll intercept any complaints from your school to your parents, okay?'

I smiled and gave a thumbs-up. I was sure Hogstein would be badgering my parents in no time.

'Master Key?'

'Yes?'

'If the twins speak to Hogstein – as my parents, I mean –' I stared at the clouds outside '– then, well . . . tell him I'm sorry.'

Master Key turned and raised his eyebrows.

'As you wish.'

I examined my papers. It was like seeing a little potted history of the week. There were the tickets from my trip: the Colosseum, the Vatican, the art galleries. There was the little codebook, *The Dough Vinci Code*. There was Fresco's pizza message, written on a scrap of paper. There was Justin's threatening note. There were even the notes on Major Marjorie, scrawled on a menu from Caesar Pizza. How distant a world Caesar Pizza seemed. How ignorant I was. For no reason at all, I read through the menu options. The Neptuna Pizza. The Achilles Meal. The Mark Anchovy. The

Deep-fried Haggis Pizza. And then it hit me. The threatening notes. *The menu.* The font of Justin's collaged lettering and the yellow paper were exactly the same as the Caesar Pizza menu:

NeXt TIMe Youll Be
SleepIng With The AnChoVies.

The *eep* from **SleepIng** had been taken from the *eep* in *Deep-fried Haggis Pizza*. The *Ne* in *NeXt* came from the *Neptuna Pizza*, while the *Me* in **TIMe** came from the *Achilles Meal*.

Justin must have swiped some menus when he took the pizza on Rufflington Beach.

I then scanned down. My brain was bubbling to life now, and it was telling me that there was still something missing. Something major. When I saw the bottom-right corner of the menu, I got it. Our address.

Caesar Pizza

113 Brayne Road

Rufflington-On-Sea

RFF1 8LT

More specifically, it was the postcode that grabbed me: RFF1 8LT. I picked up Fresco's pizza message again:

RFF1 CUT OPEN THE FISH 8LT.

When you covered the words 'cut open the fish', it was clear. RFF1 8LT. The postcode. My parents' pizzeria. It seemed impossible! A cold sweat gushed over me as I saw the two worlds collide: the world of my family, of Rufflington pizzas, a world where not very much happened. And the world of Big Alan Fresco and the G.S.L. A world of art theft, coded toppings and attempted murder.

'I know where Fresco's going!' I shouted. 'Get to Rufflington!'

A painful forty minutes passed as we flew over France. I explained my theories to the other two, who nodded grimly. I kept my eyes on the flightpath as my thoughts went crazy. What were Fresco and his mad bunch going to Caesar Pizza for? Had they actually hidden *Girl with a Squirrel* there? Or were they just plotting some sick revenge against me personally? I had horrible visions of what they would do to the place. I thought of my family, tucked up in the flat above. My dad could get angry, true, and he did have a cricket bat for bashing intruders. But it might need more than that to deal with Fresco and his big, hefty boys. I pictured the pizzeria, trashed and burgled. It would all be my fault. Would they smash the windows? Light the ovens and set fire to the place? Take down the statue of Markus Anchovius and chop it to bits? Then it struck me: Markus Anchovius. The statue of a fish. *Cut open the fish.* Could that be the hiding place for *Girl with a Squirrel*?

I looked out at the torn-paper crinkles of boats crossing the Channel. Then, like a big playmat for toy cars, Rufflington appeared below. On the clifftop sat Buckdean Hall and, out to sea, the pier. I could make out the bungalows – including the Biggs's with its Christmas decorations – and the boating lagoon east of Rufflington Beach. It was here Master Key chose to land. He had messaged Georgia, the G.S.L. driver who was waiting with the not-in-service bus.

'Caesar Pizza, please, Georgia,' said Master Key as we boarded. 'And this is kind of urgent.'

We rattled through the empty streets, past the railway arches and King Skewer, over Eight Dials Crossroads, before sweeping onto Brayne Road. It was lined with burger vans, setting up for fans from the nearby football stadium.

The shutters were down in Caesar Pizza, but as

we approached a figure crept out: Tomasi. Under one arm was a square package. In the other hand was the unmistakable glint of an axe. He didn't look like the firewood-chopping type.

Chapter 24

aster Key brought a megaphone to his lips.

'In the name of the Golden Spatula League,' he shouted, 'put down the *Girl with a Squirrel*!'

A look of white-hot rage bulged in Tomasi's eyes. He charged at the bus and thrashed the axe into the front tyre. There was a violent hiss as he wrenched it out, before hurling it through the windscreen. Shards filled the air as the axe whistled past and lodged in a seat. Then he bolted, his spidery legs launching him along the pavement.

'Stop that chef!' shouted Master Key. One of the burger vendors poked his head out, only to be punched by Tomasi and flung out. Within seconds Tomasi had revved up his van and was screeching up Brayne Road. Master Key rapped on the window of another burger van.

'G.S.L.,' was all he needed to say. The vendor jumped out, gave us the keys, and we set off behind Tomasi. In the wing mirror, I saw the other burger vans roar to life. Their headlights projected out the diamond of spatulas. The convoy was complete.

We burst along the seafront. A few football fans tried hailing us for a burger. Fat chance. We were getting closer to Tomasi. Too close. He suddenly hit the brakes and we rammed into him. There was a splintering of metal as we flung ourselves down. Tomasi leapt out, and his van screeched into a line of deckchairs and burst into flames. Then he ran towards the pier, the painting under his arm.

We followed, as the smoke billowed out, smelling of fried onions. Master Key shouted into his megaphone: 'G.S.L. alert! All stations engage!'

In the boarded-up cafés on the pier, doors began to open. Dozens of G.S.L. agents spilled out, armed with whatever foodstuffs and utensils they could lay their hands on.

They surrounded Tomasi by the fortune-teller's caravan. He was lashing out like a trapped beast, but it wasn't enough to stop the G.S.L. artillery. They pelted him with spatulas, rolling pins, bags of flour, vats of oil and huge cartons of cleaning detergent. I was surprised by how vicious it all was – but that had been the theme of the week. Somehow in the commotion the painting was hurled out like a Frisbee. It smashed through the glass doors of the nearby casino and plopped onto the carpet.

'Go! Go!' shouted Master Key.

But we weren't quick enough. A slim figure in a beret and sunglasses picked it up and tore through the slot machines. Big Alan Fresco. Or, more appropriately, Slim Alan Fresco. The casino staff were too sleepy to stop the maniac running past. He elbowed them in the face, jumped out of the back door and flew up the promenade.

Extra G.S.L. agents joined us from the other side, weaving in and out of the arcades. More food-based missiles sailed through the sky. Fresco just kept on running. You had to hand it to him – he had pulled off a pretty amazing dieting routine. It was then that I heard the helicopter. It began to spit out a rope ladder, which slapped the end of the pier. In a final flourish of confusion, Fresco then lurched into the giant bouncy castle. He didn't take his shoes off. He just bounded through the rooms, a dizzying vortex of red-and-yellow stripes. Kids at school had gone on about its inflatable

staircases and upper floors. Fresco sprang up these like a flying monkey. We kept up the chase, now reduced to Master Key, Princess and me. We were struggling. Princess and I were bashed up and tired. Master Key's slippers were slowing him down. Fresco kept on appearing, then disappearing through the endless blow-up chambers, which hissed and wheezed and squeaked as we chased. Finally, he wriggled up a turret – the outermost part of the bouncy castle, and the furthest point on the pier. As we bounced up the wobbling steps, we heard the helicopter drone louder than ever. When we reached the top, he was on the windowsill, one hand on the rope ladder. Then he brought out a knife and plunged it into the wall. There was a deafening sound of helium screaming out and the ground began to tremble. I had a moment to register Fresco jumping onto the ladder and Master Key diving after him, before the whole structure collapsed like a house of cards. We somersaulted down through the shrinking rooms. I saw Princess grab the edge of a sagging window and slither out.

'Follow me!' she shouted.

There was a *slap-slap-slap* as the last bit of ladder rose off the boardwalk. We saw Fresco climbing towards the helicopter and Master Key following, a jewel-like speck above us. We heard a *SLAP* as Fresco's hand caught Master Key's face. Then a winded *OOF* as Master Key's slipper pranged into Fresco's chest. Then the *WHOOSH* of an airborne painting, spinning down towards us.

I had a flashback of a cricket lesson, with my coach bellowing, 'WATCH THE BALL, KINGSLEY, WATCH THE BLEEDIN' BALL!' That day, the ball seemed to hang in the sky forever before accelerating down and bouncing off my fingertips. This time the opposite happened. The painting spun into my arms and I hugged it to my chest.

'Woooooooooooooooooooooo!' cried Princess.

'Noooooooooooooooooooooo!' screamed Fresco.

I then saw Brutus – or Bruno – climb down onto the rope ladder. Something glinted in his hand, like a truncheon or a club or a knife. At any rate, it wasn't a soft baguette. He approached the grappling ball of Fresco and Master Key. Almost without thinking, I brought up the purée gun and fired. There was a scream, as Brutus – or Bruno – tumbled from the rope and crashed into the sea. More shouts filled the air as Fresco slapped Master Key again and again.

'Stop! Stop!' screamed Princess.

But he didn't stop. There was a ripping sound as Master Key catapulted back, his legs tangling in the ladder. He was moving like a partially squashed insect, just about twitching with signs of life. Slowly he brought his hands up to his face and pressed his laser ring. A powerful beam scorched up towards Fresco. But the rope swayed in the wind, and the beam sped past him and onto the helicopter.

I had only seen explosions in bad action films. They always seemed massive, impossibly orange, with millions of domes of fire. This one was like that, times ten. And what the films don't convey is the heat, cooking your face even from a distance. It was like the whole sky was in a giant twisted spasm, with pieces of helicopter scattering out. Lost in all that fiery chaos were two very different people. One was an art thief and a bully. The other was the boy who only yesterday had saved my life. I sank to my knees, my vision swimming with glitchy images. A wall of foam surging up from the sea. Smoke twisting like a monstrous arm. And a shred of white, flickering for a second. It could have been a piece of propeller. Or a really dumb seagull. Or, if I chose to believe it, a parachute, trying to open.

Chapter 25

e went to King Skewer. Princess wanted me away from the police boats, the TV crews and all those questions, questions, questions. She led me to the storeroom and pressed on a jar of tahini sauce. A trapdoor opened and we climbed into her office. Golden spatulas on the wall, a pool table for a desk, rows of monitors, a mini-aquarium. Big deal. I didn't care any more.

I didn't care about fancy offices. I didn't care about the painting of some rodent no one knew the name of. All I cared about was the dot on our watch screens, pulsing for a sign of Master Key.

For so long, for too long, it just bleeped slowly and groggily, as if the watch itself was spluttering. I knew the G.S.L. could do anything. But survive that? The police had fished out Fresco – what was left of him – but nothing of Master Key. Nothing. Princess tried to reassure me, but her words came out garbled like a broken tape. Everything made us jump. The trains rumbling over the shop, King Skewer rattling with the deep-fat fryers. And then, grainy and blue like a half-developed photo, a silhouette formed on our screens.

'Well,' it purred, 'that was a bit *too* dramatic, wasn't it?'

I nearly fell off my chair. Princess said some almost-naughty words.

'What the fluff! Where are you how are you how did you –?'

'I must say, Camillo did a fine job with these watches,' said the silhouette. 'Although mine's on the blink, as you can imagine.'

'Master Key, we don't want to talk about Camillo's little toys! Tell us what the *heck* happened. Are you okay?'

'I'm fine, Princess. I've been better, and that *was* my favourite dressing gown, but you know what they say about omelettes and breaking eggs.'

Princess raised her eyebrows at me.

'Anyhow . . . I'm in the mini-sub. Honestly, I can't move too well right now, but I'll be okay. Camillo's a genius. The parachute dressing gown. The mini-sub homing in on my signal . . . and the water wasn't *that* cold, even by British summer standards. Unfortunately, what with everything . . .' The line crackled and I thought we were losing him – but it was just a very long sigh. 'The truth is,' he continued, 'I must leave the G.S.L. As you know, I'm that age now, and with everything that happened today – so public, you know – I must step down.'

This time I did fall off my chair. Princess
scowled at me.

'Friends,' he continued. 'I am so extremely
proud of you. The word "hero" was invented
for people like you. You've done something no
pizza delivery boy and kebab vendor – or anyone,
really – has ever done before. Anchovy – you will
make a fine G.S.L. detective, I know it. I've always
had faith in you.'

My lower lip did a wobble-jiggle.

'And Princess – I can't thank you enough.
You're the ultimate mentor. It's only right that you
succeed me; the approval from up top has long been
in place. You know what to do.'

Princess nodded, stunned. For once she was lost
for words.

'Now please, I insist. Do *not* try to contact me. It
will be very dangerous for everyone. You saw what
happened today.'

Sheesh, I thought.

'Well,' he sighed, muffled by the bubbles outside the mini-sub, 'I bid you farewell, friends. When the time comes, we'll meet again. *Aureum in spatha est, vivat in spatha!*'

And with that, the silhouette dissolved into blue, which shrank again to a dot, and we were left in silence beneath a kebab shop once more.

Princess went over to the fish tank.

'I knew it was coming, Anch. Just not like this.' She sprinkled some pellets into the tank. 'We're told this happens in the G.S.L. . . .' Her voice wavered and she looked away from me, towards the fish hoovering up their food. 'When it's time to leave, you must leave quickly and quietly. It will happen to me. It will happen to you.' She wiped her eyes and returned to the desk. 'Anyway – we must stick to G.S.L. protocol.'

'G.S.L. protocol?'

'Your graduation, I mean. Put your foot on the desk, please.'

I did as she said and plonked my trainers on the pool table. She opened a metal box and brought out something that looked suspiciously like a tattoo pen.

'Now, take off your shoe and sock. You are no longer an apprentice.'

'What are you doing?'

'Giving you your permanent G.S.L. tattoo, if you're okay with that.'

'I guess so.'

I peeled off the sock and Princess recoiled.

'You really need to wash more thoroughly.'

She set to work, tracing the shape of Markus Anchovius into my second toe. Underneath that, she rendered the diamond of spatulas. I could feel her cool fingers on the tips of my toes. But she didn't look bothered or embarrassed. I knew now that she had loved Master Key.

'There,' she said, and slapped a bit of clingfilm on it. 'Don't wash it or touch it for five hours, okay?'

'Okay.'

'This is your passport into virtually anywhere, you know. You're an official G.S.L. caterer detective now.'

She put the pen away and brought out some papers and two glass bottles.

'You have *become* the Mark Anchovy. Pink lemonade?'

I took a glug and studied the papers.

'Take these back, have a read, sign them and return to me this week. I won't be here after that.'

'Where are you going?'

'The London G.S.L. Headquarters. I'll be Head of the UK branch now, Anchovy.'

'Congratulations!'

'Well, it's not official yet.'

'Will I have to call you "Queen Skewer" now?'

She smiled for the first time that day.

'Maybe.'

We went over to the ladder. Next to it, cushioned on a bag of flatbreads, was the painting. That snooty girl. That ridiculous squirrel. I mean, who owns a squirrel?! I gave it one last look before we climbed out.

'I'm glad it's all over.' Princess sighed. 'There is just one more thing, though.'

Chapter 26

fter all that, it felt absurd to be in Rufflington Police Station – a place where a lost cat counted as drama. Superintendent Sandpip turned to me, her mouth in a confused wriggle.

'Imagine my surprise, Colin,' she said, gulping her tenth mug of tea, 'when a file arrived from Scotland Yard with your name on it!'

She shook her head and her black bun of hair quivered like a jelly.

'I'm not allowed to know or share details, as this appears to have been verified by a top-secret department.' She pointed to a gold-stamped logo: the G.S.L.'s diamond of spatulas.

I tried to keep an innocent look on my face – never easy in a police station.

'But it seems,' she continued after crunching a hobnob, 'that you have been excused by the highest authority for vandalising a school bus, escaping from an Italian police station, playing truant from a scheduled flight and generally – from what Mr Hogstein tells me – causing complete havoc during your school trip.'

I avoided eye contact and stared at the 'lost cat' posters behind her.

'Mr Hogstein has accepted your apologies. He understands that you have played an important role as a witness to some sort of incident in Rome.' She sighed. 'What with the explosion over the pier as well . . . it has been an eventful morning.'

She led me out, carefully stepping around the

jumbled piles of paper.

'Now, there is a certain individual who will be dealt with internally.'

Out in the corridor, Princess sat on a bench.

'This way, please,' said Sandpip, indicating the cell. We entered and I felt sick at the sight of him: Justin.

'Back off, fish-breath!' He hocked a green dollop onto my shoe.

'We have this all under control, Superintendent,' said Princess. 'Would you mind giving us a minute?'

Sandpip shrugged and left the cell.

Princess turned to Justin.

'Listen, you little fluff-chomper, either you tell us everything or you'll be getting the mother of all wedgies in a juvenile detention centre.'

His beady eyes narrowed behind his wispy fringe.

'I'm not bothered! I'd do it again! I'd destroy all of you!'

He hocked another phlegmy missile, but my dodging skills had sharpened.

'Just tell us why, Juice Box,' muttered Princess. 'Why did you fluff us over?'

He huffed.

'I snuck into Pizza-face's suitcase because I wanted to help. And I could have helped! I'm way better than him! Anyway . . . you guys were all like, "Stay here, little baby Juice Box, and keep out of trouble . . . " But I wasn't taking that, no, not me. Not Juice Box!'

He puffed his chest out, getting all cocky.

'It was sooooo easy. La Casa Bianca was slap bang next door, so I just went to Tomasi and spilled the beans. Fresco was already under house arrest and they'd set up the pizza code, so we had to stick to that, obvs. Then they came to get me and burnt down Camillo's little nerd-cave.'

He gave a gruesome snigger, like a coughing pug.

'I told them all about you, Pizza-face,' he sneered at me. 'Your hotel, where they could find you, how they could get you *whacked*, you know.'

He waved his little mitts around.

'What happened with the painting?' I asked.

He licked his lips.

'Fresco knew everyone would trust a sweet little boy like me. The guys at the airport didn't even bat an eyelid!'

Princess rubbed her eyes.

'Then I hid it at Pizza-face's place, didn't I? Last place he'd look!'

'What did you do to Markus Anchovius?'

'Oh, you mean that big ugly fishy-wish your parents made? Ha!'

I felt like pointing the purée gun in his face, but didn't.

'You lot never heard about my special skill, did you?' he grinned. 'Lock-picking.'

About Markus Anchovius: I've already
mentioned the coin slit in his mouth. Well, these
coins collect in a biggish old base, under his tail.
On this base is a door, and on this door is a lock. A
paperclip could open it. Not 'special skill'.

'Honestly, Pizza-face,' Justin scoffed, 'it was

boooooring how simple it was.
Tomasi wasn't so gentle with it
though, haha!'

His sneery tone was pushing
all the wrong buttons, and I
boiled over.

'So what was in it for *you* then,
Juice Box?' I snapped.

'Well . . . I nipped back to
Italy didn't I? I knew that the lads
couldn't do without *me*.'

His whole face went droopy.

'Fresco said he'd fake his

293

death, pick up the painting, sell it and split the 20 mill with me.'

A snail-trail of snot left his nostril. I offered him a tissue.

'B-b-but . . .' he sniffled, 'he lied to me!!!'

'Of course he did, you doofus!' shouted Princess. 'No one with half a brain cell would trust a man like Fresco!'

Justin stopped sniffling. A furious glint came into his eyes. He stood on the bench and raised his little fist to the ceiling.

'DOWN WITH THE G.S.L.!' he shouted. 'DOWN WITH THE G.S.L.!'

Princess sighed and led me out.

'You can take him away now,' she said to Superintendent Sandpip.

We trundled out and into Rufflington, with its doll-house streets and ruler-straight hedges.

Princess put her hand on my shoulder. 'You did well, Anchovy. Really well. You'll make a fluffing good detective.'

'Will I get a secret office like yours?'

'Yup. It's in the new contract. Camillo will fit one out under Caesar Pizza for you. Anyway – you need to get yourself home.'

We approached the hill over the Eight Dials Crossroads, the salty breeze on our cheeks.

We shook hands – hers all calloused, mine strangely soft.

'Goodbye for now, Anchovy.'

'Thank you, Princess Skewer,' I said. 'Let me know if you need me for anything.'

'I will. See you around, Pizza-head.'

I walked back, clutching my new G.S.L. contract. An official caterer detective.

I skimmed through the clauses as my tired legs took me home. The numbers concerning my payments made my head spin. I imagined my secret office – perhaps I could get a hot tub in there.

Eventually I was back on Brayne Road. With the sun rising, seagulls cawing and dog walkers bagging up poo, I felt like I had returned to normality.

In the window of Caesar Pizza, I could see my mum taking out the toppings from the fridge.

My dad was trying to patch up poor Markus Anchovius. He saw me first, and his stubbly face broke into a smile.

'The jet-setter returns!' he called. 'Boy, have you missed some drama here!' He gave me a hug, as my mum dropped the toppings in alarm.

'Colin!' she squealed, and muscled in on the hug. 'You look shattered!'

'I am,' I croaked, tears finally welling up in my eyes. She patted down the collar of the trench coat. She called Alicia, who jumped down the stairs

 two at a time and head-butted my stomach as she hugged my waist.

'Is that my little Bogey?' rasped a voice from around the corner.

'G-pops!'

He was by the ice-cream counter, feeding half a Flake to Dinnergloves.

'Er, G-pops, you're putting ketchup on the ice cream again.'

'So I am, lad, so I am. Well, how was Rome?'

'Oh, it was . . .'

'Beautiful?'

I nodded. It *was* beautiful – and I had barely stopped to look at it.

'Did you see the Sistine Chapel?'

'Yeah, there was a weird bit of floppy skin up there that was quite . . . inspiring.'

'And the Colosseum?'

'Oh, that was intense . . .'

'And the Trevi Fountain? Did you get up close to that?'

'Very close. Too close, maybe.'

'Colin, you're the luckiest boy in the world. I hope you know that.' He slurped his ketchup-covered ice cream without a grimace. 'Did you make any nice friends?'

A lump formed in my throat.

'Super-nice friends. But . . . I don't know when I'll see them again.'

'I know, Colin, I know how you're feeling. Friends are so important. If you can think of each other as often as you can and remember all those moments, you'll never lose your friends.'

'Did you ever go to Rome, G-pops?'

'I wish!'

The room was then filled with the salty-fishy waft of a Mark Anchovy pizza. My dad brought it out and sliced it up on one of the boxes. Then we all sat down at the small table in the back, with a swig of coke to balance out the saltiness.

'We've missed you, Colin.'

I smiled and wiped away a stringy beard of cheese that was forming on my chin.

'I've missed you, too.'

Acknowledgements

A big thank you to: David Thomas, for getting
the ball rolling; Lynsey Rogers and Will Mackie
for their early support on the Scottish Book Trust
mentorship scheme; Pamela Butchart, for all
her insight, energy and honesty; Tessa David, a
wonderful agent without whom Mark Anchovy
would be languishing in a drawer; Jane Harris,
Felicity Alexander, Sophie McDonnell and all
at Bonnier for championing this book – and for
their patience.

Lastly to my kind, loving family, who don't run
an Ancient Rome-themed pizzeria.

Take a sneak peek at Mark Anchovy's next
adventure with the Golden Spatula League . . .

MARK ANCHOVY

WAR & PIZZA

Chapter 1

y employers, the Golden Spatula League, promise their detectives both luxury and danger.

Interpreting 'luxury' as a secret office with a hot tub, I glossed over the 'danger' part. I didn't think I'd be chased by an actual wolf. Or get ejected from a plane. Or have my eyebrows singed off. Plus, there was no hot tub. If I'd known then what I know now, I might never have answered the pizza-phone, as it angrily tootled one night in December.

'Yes?'

'Since when is "yes?" how you answer the phone to a superior?'

It was my boss, Princess Skewer. Skewer, because of the kebabs she sells. Princess, because she acts like one.

'I mean . . . Mark Anchovy spea—'

'Did you get the assignment?'

'Which assignment?'

I capsized the tower of light-blue envelopes sprouting from my desk. My training had recently gone from intensive to turbo. Here was a questionnaire on the league's founding; here were certificates for elementary contortion, calligraphy, fencing. Here was a pamphlet titled *How to Spot a Criminal of the Catering Underworld*.

'Anchovy. If you plan to stay in a G.S.L. job – which many would give their right arm for –' I'm left-handed, so this was lost on me – 'I suggest you get a filing system.'

She sounded just like Mr Hogstein, my crusty history teacher.

'It's okay, I've found it.'

'There's no time. Head up to Caesar Pizza. Over and out.'

No sooner had I twisted the tomato can that activated the revolving wall, shot up the ladder and casually strolled into my parents' pizzeria, than the main line rang.

My mum answered in her super polite, high-pitched voice.

'Yes-yes, yes-yes, a Mark Anchovy pizza with *extra* anchovies? Yes-yes, yes-yes, right away.'

My dad's monobrow wiggled like a belly-dancing slug. He picked up a rolling pin and set to work.

'Odd,' said my mum, grating the mozzarella. 'He wants it delivered to a houseboat.'

Something tugged on my apron. Something

with a wonky fringe and laser-like gaze: Alicia, my sister.

'Colinnnnnnnnnnnnnnn,' she chanted. 'Who were you talking to in the storeroom?'

'Er . . . myself.'

'Yourself?'

'Uh-huh.'

'Right. I thought you were, you know, talking to friends or practising your lines for that arty-farty school play. But you were talking to yourself?'

'Yep.'

'Wierrrrdooooooooooo!!'

She climbed onto a high-stool and began shredding napkins. When Alicia wasn't climbing things she was cutting things. Like her own hair. Or family albums. Or *my* comics. And when she wasn't doing this she was twanging a double-bass, when tinkling a nice, quiet triangle would have been fine for everyone.

The cheesy, salty-fishy waft of a cooked Mark Anchovy pizza tickled my nostrils.

'No faffing,' was my dad's pearl of wisdom as he packed up the pizza.

'Is your bike light working?' fretted my mum.

Considering what lay ahead, worrying about a bike light was like questioning your choice of swimming trunks in the face of a tsunami.

Apart from a seagull maiming a bin-bag, the streets were empty. I left town via Saltpan Lane – that long dark gullet of which Rufflington is the waste-hole. I passed the abandoned windmill, its tired sails groaning. River reeds moshed. Mud replaced tarmac. Marsh replaced mud. Finally, in the bottle-green blackness, the light of a boat bobbed up ahead. I sludged down the bank. My pizza-watch beeped with instructions from Princess:

Deliver the pizza, recky the place and get out. P.S.

I drew up the collar of my trench coat – well, my mum's trench coat – and rapped on a porthole.

No answer. I caught the tinkle of a radio and a kettle reaching boiling point. It wasn't the only one. Dodging a scabby rope, I knocked on the cabin's hobbit-door.

'Mark Anchovy pizza!' I scanned my mum's note. 'For a Mr . . . Cinnamon Ben?' Was that even a name? 'Helloooooooo???!!!' Nothing. Apparently we now delivered pizzas to corpses. I heaved a sigh and opened the door. It was a narrow, coffin-like space, with a knotty pine table and a mounted lamp. Opposite this was a cuckoo-clock, of all things. A saucepan was bubbling on a dinky oven-top. Inside, an egg was going berserk. And on the sideboard lay a chipped, flowery plate, with fingers of toast spread like sunbeams. A boiled egg and soldiers? *And* pizza? Was Cinnamon Ben some kind of unstoppable eating machine? I went a-reckying.

There was a bathroom with a bucket, and a bar of soap that looked like it would actually make you dirtier. There was a cabinet with brown glass pill-bottles. A bedroom, with a fat fur-coat on a skinny bed. An old brick phone. A book on antiques. A pamphlet with the title *Baltic Cruises*. An empty, teal-coloured glasses case that snapped like a clam. A torn sepia photograph of some kids at the seaside. And a postcard of a church, written in an alphabet I couldn't read. This, I pocketed. There was nothing in the way of a wallet. And nothing in the way of Cinnamon Ben.

Well??? beeped Princess.

I returned to the main cabin. I needed to sit – and eat – and think about all this. If there was a newly boiled egg, a phone, a fur coat, then this hungry, loopy old antique-lover couldn't have got far. I opened the satchel and took a slice of pizza. An anchovy plopped off and I bent down to get it.

But when I came up, the slice of pizza where my head had just been was now a mere crust. The rest of the slice was splatted on the wall behind me, in several explosive blobs. It was pinned there by an arrow.

Earth to Anchovy???!! Princess beeped again with impeccable timing. My mission in Rome taught me that when pizzas explode where your head just was, you don't reply to a text message. You duck under a table and reach for your molten tomato purée gun. Any worries I used to have about using this deadly weapon vanished.

Cycling along a marsh in winter, delivering a pizza, getting no tips, being interrupted while eating, and now assassination! Who did this Cinnamon Ben think he was? I stuck out a hand and fired a jet of lava-like tomato. There was a *hiss* as it scorched a hole somewhere. Then that cartoonish squeak again. I jutted out an eyebrow.

It was the cuckoo clock. Something was winding out. Only it wasn't a merry little wooden bird. It was some kind of mechanically powered crossbow. Pointed at *me*. I just ducked in time. *THUNK!* went the arrow. The raggedy bits of pizza took another pasting. *THUNK!* went another arrow. The pizza-bits rained down. *THUNK!* went a third arrow. An olive beetled down my neck. I had to stop that clock! I slid on my belly and molten-tomatoed it from the end of the table. The good news was that it clogged up the machinery. The bad news was that the lamp exploded. It was too fast to take everything in, but I think it sparked, and these sparks decided to bounce all over the oven. It would have been very simple to have turned off the gas when I looked in the pan. But I didn't. And we all know what happens when a spark meets a lit gas-hob. They get on like a houseboat on fire. The next thing I knew was that the space – appropriately, as I mentioned, being of coffin-width – was filling up with smoke. Not wanting to be left out, a few tea-towels had also lent themselves to the inferno.

Erm . . . message me please???!! Princess rat-a-tatted on my watch.

Can't talk right now . . . I'm kind of being assassinated by a booby-trapped boat, I tapped back. I immediately regretted my lack of economy. The flames were now breakdancing in a hot orange cyclone on the floor. I got off my belly and made for the hobbit-door. But as soon as I stood up I was flung back down. The boat was spinning. Spinning, I realised, because it was no longer tied to the bank. Which meant that this floating incinerator was in the middle of a river with only one very wet means of exit. Sometimes, on long car journeys, after she's stolen my last fruit pastille (always a black one) Alicia and I ask each other random questions like,

'would you rather burn to death or freeze to death?'
It now seemed I was a fan of the second option.
Somehow, I charged out of the spinning cabin,
didn't puke, dodged a wall of fire, and jumped into
the river, trench coat and all. When I'd emptied my
eyeballs of algae, I watched the burning carcass slip
below the surface. Whatever evidence I could have
gathered about Cinnamon Ben was wasted. Along
with a perfectly good pizza.